"How long do you figure it will be before we end up in bed together again?"

The sheer arrogance of Colin's question should have annoyed her, but his words—and the images they evoked—sent a quick thrill through her. But she couldn't let him kiss her again, because if he did, she knew she'd be lost.

"You…uh…really need to go," she said, just a little breathlessly.

Then his lips were on hers and all thoughts of further protest evaporated.

This was crazy. It was wrong. He wouldn't stay in town for the long term. He never did. Maybe he'd come back occasionally now that he knew about Carly, but she couldn't hope for any more than that. He'd already broken her heart once before. She could not—would not—give him that power over her again.

Dear Reader,

As always, Silhouette Intimate Moments is coming your way with six fabulously exciting romances this month, starting with bestselling Merline Lovelace, who always has *The Right Stuff*. This month she concludes her latest miniseries, TO PROTECT AND DEFEND, and you'll definitely want to be there for what promises to be a slam-bang finale.

Next, pay another visit to HEARTBREAK CANYON, where award winner Marilyn Pappano knows *One True Thing*: that the love between Cassidy McRae and Jace Barnett is meant to be, despite the lies she's forced to tell. Lyn Stone begins a wonderful new miniseries with *Down to the Wire*. Follow DEA agent Joe Corda to South America, where he falls in love—and so will you, with all the SPECIAL OPS. Brenda Harlen proves that sometimes *Extreme Measures* are the only way to convince your once-and-only love— and the child you never knew!—that this time you're home to stay. When *Darkness Calls*, Caridad Piñeiro's hero comes out to…slay? Not exactly, but he *is* a vampire, and just the kind of bad boy to win the heart of an FBI agent with a taste for danger. Finally, let new author Diana Duncan introduce you to a *Bulletproof Bride*, who quickly comes to realize that her kidnapper is not what he seems—and is a far better match than the fiancé she was just about to marry.

Enjoy them all—and come back next month for more of the best and most exciting romance reading around, right here in Silhouette Intimate Moments.

Yours,

Leslie J. Wainger
Executive Editor

Please address questions and book requests to:
Silhouette Reader Service
U.S.: 3010 Walden Ave., P.O. Box 1325, Buffalo, NY 14269
Canadian: P.O. Box 609, Fort Erie, Ont. L2A 5X3

Extreme
Measures
BRENDA HARLEN

INTIMATE MOMENTS™

Published by Silhouette Books

America's Publisher of Contemporary Romance

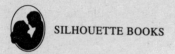 SILHOUETTE BOOKS

ISBN 0-373-27352-5

EXTREME MEASURES

Copyright © 2004 by Brenda Harlen

Visit Silhouette at www.eHarlequin.com

Printed in U.S.A.

Books by Brenda Harlen

Silhouette Intimate Moments

McIver's Mission #1224
Some Kind of Hero #1246
Extreme Measures #1282

BRENDA HARLEN

grew up in a small town surrounded by books and imaginary friends. Although she always dreamed of being a writer, she chose to follow a more traditional career path first. After two years of practicing as an attorney (including an appearance in front of the Supreme Court of Canada), she gave up her "real" job to be a mom and try her hand at writing books. Three years, five manuscripts and another baby later, she sold her first book—an RWA Golden Heart Winner—to Silhouette.

Brenda lives in southern Ontario with her real-life husband/hero, two heroes-in-training and two neurotic dogs. She is still surrounded by books ("too many books," according to her children) and imaginary friends, but she also enjoys communicating with "real" people. Readers can contact Brenda by e-mail at brendaharlen@yahoo.com or by snail mail c/o Silhouette Books, 233 Broadway, Suite 1001, New York, NY 10279.

For Angela Muirhead
(aka "Joanie")
Because our friendship started
a long time ago at a hockey game.

And with thanks to:

My brother, Jim, for stories and
insights from the dressing room.

My husband, Neill, for research
on explosives...and other things.

And Leslie Wainger and Susan Litman,
for giving this story a chance,
and helping to make it better.

Chapter 1

Colin McIver was back and Nikki Gordon was probably the only person in all of Fairweather, Pennsylvania, who wasn't thrilled about the return of the hometown hero. Of course, no one else had the questionable privilege of being his ex-wife.

Why was he back?

She crossed the parking lot of the sports' injuries clinic, scanning the article in the local newspaper she'd swiped from the staff room.

Why now?

"Hello, Nicole."

She stopped in her tracks, her eyes still fixed on the paper in her hand although the tiny black letters blurred together. She knew that voice. It didn't matter that she hadn't heard it in over five years, she'd recognize it anywhere—that deep, warm tone with the underlying sensuality that still caused tingles of anticipation to dance over her skin.

But even if she hadn't recognized the voice, she would

still have known it was him. He was the only person who ever called her Nicole, and just the sound of her name on his lips was enough to bring the memories flooding back. Memories she'd tried for so long to forget.

Her heart thudded heavily in her chest, but she glanced up with forced nonchalance into familiar deep green eyes. His dark hair was cut short, his square jaw freshly shaven, his lips tipped up at the corners. His shoulders looked as broad as she remembered, the cotton shirt he wore stretched over his powerful muscles. His waist was still trim, his denim-clad legs long and lean.

He bore the usual scars of an athlete. The slightly crooked nose that had been broken three times, the small scar that slashed through one thick eyebrow, and the barely noticeable chip in his front tooth. Yet he was still the most devastatingly handsome man she'd ever met.

It had been more than five years since she'd seen him, and she hadn't forgotten a single detail.

"Hello, Colin."

He smiled at her, a slow, curving of the lips that caused her pulse to trip, then race.

"You look good," he said, his eyes skimming over her. "You've cut your hair."

Nikki laughed and self-consciously tucked an errant strand behind her ear. She'd had hair that fell to her waist when she and Colin were married, and he'd loved to comb his fingers through it, spread it out over the pillow—

She thrust the painfully sweet memory aside. "A long time ago."

He tilted his head. "I like it."

"What are you doing here, Colin?"

"Here—in Fairweather? Or here—here?"

"Both."

"I'm here—" he indicated the physical space beside

her parked car "—because I wanted to let you know I was back."

Knowing how anxious he'd been to flee the confines of the town—and their marriage—she was more than a little surprised by his return. And completely unnerved by his sudden and unexpected appearance here. It was one thing to know he was in Fairweather, and quite another to be face-to-face with him again. "Thanks for the warning, but the press beat you to it."

He took the newspaper she held out, winced as he scanned the headline. "'Hometown Hero,' huh? I guess nothing much has changed around here if this is what passes for news."

"What did you expect?"

He studied her for a long moment. Nikki refused to shift her feet or cross her arms. She didn't want to appear annoyed or impatient, just disinterested. Anything else might suggest she had some residual feelings for Colin, and nothing could be further from the truth. There had been a time when she'd loved him more than she'd ever thought possible, but that time was long past.

"I don't know what I expected," he said at last.

She forced a polite smile. "Do you plan on staying long?"

He shrugged. "A few days, anyway."

A few days. She exhaled slowly. Whatever the reason for his return, he'd be gone in a few days and her life would settle back to normal again. Still, his presence here now made her uneasy. "Well, it was nice seeing you. Enjoy your stay."

She started past him, halting abruptly when he reached out to put a restraining hand on her arm. The touch burned her skin, and she pulled away as if he had branded her with a hot iron.

"I need to talk to you, Nicole."

She forced herself to swallow the fear that lodged in

her throat. Why was he doing this? After more than five years of silence, why did he suddenly want to talk? Had he somehow found out—

No. She trampled that thought before it had completely formed. Whatever his reasons for coming back now, they were undoubtedly as selfish and self-centered as the reasons for everything else he'd ever done.

"I know I owe you an explanation," he said.

She shook her head again. "Five years ago, I might have agreed. But too much time has passed for it to matter anymore."

"Do you expect me to believe that you never think about what we meant to each other?"

"I don't care what you believe, but I don't spend my days reminiscing about our short-lived marriage." She didn't have time to think about what they'd once had or what might have been. She was too busy dealing with the reality of what was.

"I think about it," he said. "A lot."

The intensity in his eyes made her heart stutter. She steeled her resolve. "Is there a point to this, Colin?"

"I don't want you to think that I didn't care."

"Why would I think that? Because you petitioned for divorce before our first anniversary? Or maybe because you made love to me the night before you walked out on me forever?"

She thought she saw a flicker of something in the depths of his green eyes. Hurt? Regret? She dismissed the thought.

"I had my reasons."

"I'm sure you did." She couldn't quite mask the pain and bitterness that tinged her words. He had shattered her heart when he'd walked out on their marriage, and she couldn't pretend otherwise. "I imagine it was quite inconvenient to be legally tied to a woman who lived halfway across the country."

"Dammit, Nicole. I'm not going to let you believe our marriage was an inconvenience."

She shrugged, as if it didn't matter. As if this conversation didn't bother her. As if his easy disregard of their marriage vows didn't still hurt.

"All I'm asking for is a little of your time. Half an hour."

The last thing she needed—or wanted—was to spend a single minute more with him, never mind thirty of them.

"Please, Nicole."

She closed her eyes, willed herself not to respond to the quiet plea in his voice. She wanted to say no—firmly and finally—and walk away. But she couldn't deny that there was a part of her that was curious to know why he'd tracked her down. After five years, there was still so much that she didn't know. So much that *he* didn't know.

"Half an hour," she relented.

His quick smile did crazy things to her pulse again.

"Why don't we go somewhere to grab a coffee?" he suggested.

"There's a little café across the street," Nikki told him. "I'll meet you there after I make a quick phone call."

Colin hesitated, then nodded.

Nikki waited until he was out of earshot before digging her cell phone out of her purse. She exhaled a sigh of relief when a familiar voice answered at the other end.

"Arden, I need a favor…"

It was only as he reached for the door of the restaurant that Colin realized he still held Nikki's newspaper in his hand. He glanced at the headline again.

"Get out of town for a while," Detective Brock had advised. "Go somewhere quiet. Keep a low profile."

Good advice, but how the hell was he supposed to keep a low profile when the local media still believed he was some kind of superstar?

Colin knew better. The reality was that he'd failed at everything that had ever mattered. He'd failed as a player and a coach, and he'd failed to be the kind of husband Nikki deserved.

He shoved the paper into the garbage can and headed toward the counter, wondering if his careful planning had been compromised by that seemingly harmless headline.

He'd put his plan into action forty-eight hours earlier. The first step was a flight from Texas to Maryland, where he'd reserved a room in his own name at the Baltimore Courtland Hotel. He'd taken a cab from the airport to the hotel and checked into his room, with explicit instructions that he did not want housekeeping services. After unpacking some clothing and toiletries, he'd taken another cab to the bus terminal and paid cash for a ticket to Washington, D.C.

In Washington, he'd picked up the rental car his agent, Ian Edwards, had reserved for him. Then he'd found a small roadside motel, paid cash for the room and crashed for a few hours before driving through to Fairweather yesterday morning, where he'd checked into another Courtland hotel under Ian's name.

He wasn't convinced the circuitous route and subterfuge were necessary, but after what had happened in Austin he didn't want to take any chances. If someone was looking for him, trying to track his moves, they'd be concentrating on the Baltimore area.

Unless they happened to pick up a copy of the *Fairweather Gazette*.

He'd told no one of his plan to return to Fairweather. It was just his bad luck that he'd run into Traci Harper as soon as he'd arrived in town yesterday afternoon. Traci was an old high-school friend, now a reporter with the

Gazette. He should have anticipated that she would some-how turn a chance encounter into a news item.

His only consolation was that it was unlikely anyone outside of this smack-in-the-middle-of-nowhere town read the local rag. Few of his associates even knew he'd grown up in Fairweather, which made it the obvious place for him to find solitude and anonymity.

Or maybe what he'd really wanted to find was Nikki.

He took the two steaming mugs to a vacant table near the window, where he could see her.

He hadn't let himself think about her until he was on the plane; he hadn't been able to think about anything else since. After more than five years, he wouldn't have expected that she'd figure so prominently in his thoughts.

Maybe it was the realization that he could have been killed, the stark reminder of his own mortality. Whatever the reason, he'd suddenly felt a compelling need to see her again—to explain something he still wasn't sure he understood himself.

He watched as she disconnected her call, tucked the phone back into her purse. As she crossed the street, her short blond hair bobbed with each step.

She was dressed in casual work attire: short-sleeved sweater in a misty shade of blue, tailored pants a few shades darker, white running shoes. It wasn't a seductive outfit by any stretch of the imagination, but he felt the familiar tug of desire, anyway. Just like the first time he'd seen her.

He'd fought it at first, refused to believe it. The coolly reserved, completely professional physiotherapist wasn't anything at all like the women he was usually attracted to. But something inside him had recognized her as his mate.

He'd pursued her relentlessly, and when he'd finally broken through her barriers, he'd found an incredibly passionate woman—a woman who'd touched him on levels he hadn't known existed before he met her. Whatever else might have gone wrong between them, the sex had always been phenomenal.

He shifted in his seat, cursing his body for choosing to remember that now.

"Thirty minutes," she reminded him, sliding into the chair across from him.

He pushed one of the mugs toward her. "A little bit of cream, a half a teaspoon of sugar." He'd remembered her preference, as he'd remembered everything about her.

She wrapped her hands around the mug, a wry smile curving her lips. "It's been five years. A lot of things have changed in that time."

"Some things never do," he countered.

"Are you going to tell me the real reason you came back to Fairweather now?"

"You always did cut right to the chase." It was one of the things he'd admired about her from the start. She'd been the first therapist assigned to work with him after the injury that had prematurely ended his career, and he'd always appreciated her straightforward approach—even when she was telling him things he didn't want to hear.

"So why are you here?"

"I was ready for a vacation?" he suggested.

"And you chose Fairweather?" Her eyes narrowed speculatively. "Or is your sudden reappearance somehow linked to the explosion in your apartment?"

Talk about cutting to the chase. "How did you know about that?"

"It was on the news."

Colin had caught mention of it himself during the previous evening's sports highlights. The commentary was brief, mentioning only that police were investigating a suspected bombing at the residence of Tornadoes' head coach Colin McIver. There was no mention of Maria Vasquez, the forty-seven-year-old mother of five, who'd been cleaning his apartment at the time and who was still fighting for her life in ICU.

"Was it a gas leak?" Nikki asked.

He only wished the explanation was something so innocuous. "The cause is still being investigated."

"Is that why you're here?"

"My apartment needs a little work," he said, deliberately downplaying the situation. "But that's only part of the reason that I decided to come back now."

"And the other part?"

"To see you."

She stared intently into her cup for a long moment before lifting her gaze. "Why?"

"Because I've spent some time in the past few weeks reevaluating my life, facing my mistakes, acknowledging my regrets."

Her smile was sad. "Where do I fit in? A mistake? Or a regret?"

He reached across the table and covered her hand with his own. "The mistake was in letting you go."

"You say that as if *I* wanted out of our marriage, but *you* were the one who left. *You* were the one who wanted the divorce."

"I was too screwed up to know what I wanted. After my father died…" He shrugged.

"I know his death was hard on you," she said gently. "I know you wished you'd had a chance to bridge the distance between the two of you."

"I tried. I guess I just didn't try hard enough." The sense of regret, of guilt, still gnawed at him. "Did I ever tell you about the last conversation I had with him?"

She shook her head. "What happened?"

"We argued." He smiled wryly. "It seemed like we were *always* arguing about something. This time it was about you."

"Me?"

"He wanted—no, he demanded—that I give up coaching. He said it was past time for me to quit chasing a
dream, to get a real job, to be the kind of husband you
deserved."

Richard McIver had berated Colin for even considering
the coaching job, insisting that a woman like Nikki
needed security and stability, not the kind of nomad existence his career would entail.

But without his career, Colin had nothing to offer his
wife. So he'd taken the job, she'd stayed in Fairweather,
and their marriage had become a casualty of geographical
distance.

And his father had died as he'd lived: angry with and
disappointed in his youngest son.

"I'm sorry, Colin."

"So am I," he said. "About so many things."

He rubbed his thumb over her third finger, where his
ring had once sat. "I thought you would have married
again."

She tugged her hand, but he didn't release his hold.

"And I thought 'till death do us part' meant something
longer than ten months."

He winced at the direct hit. "I guess I deserved that."

"What do you want me to say, Colin? Do you want
me to tell you that there's no one else in my life because
I haven't been able to forget about you? Well, I haven't.
I haven't forgotten how devastated I was when you
walked out on me, and I won't ever risk going through
that again."

"I am sorry."

She shrugged off his apology, glanced at her watch.
"Your half hour's almost up."

Colin pushed back his chair and rose to his feet with
her. He knew he should be grateful she'd even been willing to sit down and have a conversation with him. After

five years, it was more than he'd had a right to expect. But it wasn't nearly enough.

- He walked with her across the street back to the clinic parking lot. She stopped beside her car, turned to face him. "Thanks for the coffee."

So this was it then—the brush-off. He'd expected it, but he wasn't prepared for it. He couldn't—wouldn't—believe that there was nothing left for them.

Testing her, maybe testing himself, he lifted his hand to tuck a stray lock of hair behind her ear and allowed his fingers to graze her cheek as he pulled back. He heard her sharp intake of breath, knew the casual contact had sparked something inside her. It had sure as hell stoked the fire that burned inside him.

"Is it really so easy to walk away?" he asked.

The warmth in her eyes cooled considerably. "You tell me."

"No." He dropped his hands to her slender waist, struggled against the impulse to pull her tight against his body. Events of the past few days had shown Colin how short life could be, and he didn't want to waste any more time. He also knew if he moved too fast, he'd scare her off. "Leaving you was the hardest thing I've ever done."

"But you did it."

"I thought it was the best thing for both of us." He stroked his hands down over her hips slowly, then back to her waist, his thumbs skimming her ribs. "Now I know I was wrong. Because even after five years, I can't forget the way it was between us."

"That was a long time ago, Colin."

"It could be like that again."

She started to shake her head.

He didn't want to hear the protest he knew was coming, so he silenced her the most effective way he knew—with his mouth.

He felt her stiffen, but she didn't pull away. In fact,

her eyelids had just started to lower when the shrill ring of his cell phone intruded.

Later that evening, as Nikki sat alone on the front porch of her home, she would admit—if only to herself—that she'd never experienced with another man the kind of desire she'd felt just being held by Colin. The simple anticipation of his kiss had heated her blood more quickly and completely than any other man's kisses ever had.

The physical attraction worried her. She'd never been the type of woman to let her hormones overrule her common sense. Except with Colin. The only man who could make her heart soar with a simple look, an innocent touch, was the only man who'd ever broken that same heart.

The thought terrified her, as did the realization that there was so much more at stake than just her heart this time.

She'd always known it was possible that he might come back someday. But it had been a remote concern, almost unreal, so long as he was halfway across the country. Now that he was here, she knew it was time to face the deception she'd lived with every day for the past five years.

She had to tell him. She couldn't keep the secret any longer—she wasn't sure she even wanted to. But knowing what she had to do didn't make it any easier to find the right words.

Colin, you have a child.

It sounded simple enough, except that Carly was *her* child. Nikki was the one who'd been there every day of Carly's life: when she'd cut her first tooth, taken her first step. She'd been the one to sit up with Carly through sleepless nights, to kiss her scraped knees, to worry over every cough and fever.

Still, she knew that biology gave him certain rights,

not the least of which was the right to know he'd fathered a child. She had wanted to tell him about Carly years ago. She'd wanted to save her marriage, to be with the man she'd loved, but she'd refused to use their baby to do so. She'd loved Colin fiercely, completely, and it would have devastated her to know that he'd only stayed with her for their daughter.

So she'd kept her pregnancy a secret, consented to the divorce, and a few months later, she'd given birth to Carly.

Now he was back, and everything seemed to be spinning out of her control.

She heard the sound of a car approaching, breathed a sigh of relief that Arden was finally home from her meeting at the women's shelter. Arden Doherty was her cousin, her roommate, and her best friend. And she was the only person Nikki could talk to about the chaos that had come to town with her ex-husband.

Nikki turned around as the vehicle pulled into the driveway. Her heart pounded frantically against her ribs as she realized it wasn't Arden's car. And it wasn't her cousin who got out of the car.

It was Colin.

Her easy smile froze; panic clawed at her throat.

The shock of finding Colin outside the clinic where she worked didn't compare to the sense of terror building inside as he moved toward the front porch of the house where she lived. Where their little girl was sleeping inside.

What was he doing here?

And more importantly, how quickly could she get him to leave?

She fought against the panic, forced her tone to remain neutral. ''What are you doing here?''

He stepped onto the porch, leaned a shoulder against

one of the upright posts. "Haven't we already had this conversation today?"

"And didn't we say everything we needed to say?" she countered.

He took a step closer, deliberately invading her personal space. "I think we have some unfinished business."

His gaze dropped to her lips, and she knew he was thinking about kissing her again. Just as she knew she couldn't let it happen.

She lifted her hands to his chest, intent on pushing him away. She could feel the heat of his skin through his shirt, the unyielding strength of his muscles, the thunderous beating of his heart.

"It's been a really long day and I have to get up early in the morning and I'm sure you have things to do and if you want to get together for coffee some time on the weekend maybe we could do that, but now really isn't…"

Her words trailed off as he skimmed his knuckles down her cheek.

"You babble when you're nervous." His lips curved in a slow, seductive smile that made her breath catch in her throat and her pulse race. "I like that I can still make you nervous."

She could hardly deny it. Nor could she deny the anticipation that surged through her veins as his head lowered toward her.

Then his mouth closed over hers and a wave of desire crashed through the last, lingering vestiges of her resistance. Overwhelmed by yearning, overpowered by need, she closed her eyes and surrendered to the sweet, mindless pleasure of his kiss.

His lips were as masterful as she remembered. She'd never known anyone who could kiss like Colin, with a kind of arrogant confidence that might have been annoying if it wasn't so darned arousing.

Her lips parted on a sigh to welcome the teasing caress of his tongue as he deepened the kiss. She hadn't felt his arms come around her, hadn't been aware of her own reaching for him, but suddenly they were entwined together and the press of his long, lean and very hard body sent dangerous currents racing through her. She shifted closer, the friction of the subtle movement making her skin burn, her body ache.

It had been years—five years, in fact—since she'd felt anything close to this kind of arousal. And all it took was a kiss.

Or maybe it was Colin.

She had no defenses against him. She never had. It was this fleeting thought, this reminder of their disastrous history, that finally penetrated the sensual haze fogging her brain and jolted her back to reality.

She pulled out of his arms. "I want you to go, Colin."

"Making me leave isn't going to make the attraction between us go away." He brushed his thumb over the curve of her bottom lip, moist and swollen from his kiss. "The chemistry's still there. You might not like it, but you can't deny it."

He was right—she couldn't deny it. But she could, and she would, resist it. What was chemistry without staying power, anyway? Nothing more than an invitation to heartbreak—and she'd been there, done that.

She took a deliberate step back. "I have no intention of being a distraction for you while you're in town."

"Do you think that's all I want?"

"I gave up trying to figure out what you wanted a long time ago."

He moved toward her, breaching the careful distance she'd put between them. "I want you, Nicole. I've always wanted you."

Her heart did a silly little flip-flop inside her chest, but she refused to show how much his words affected her. "What about me?" she countered. "What about what *I* want?"

"Tell me," he said, his voice as seductive as a caress. "Tell me what you want."

She steeled herself against the traitorous yearnings of her body, the inexplicable longing in her heart.

I want you to go.

Before she could speak, the familiar creak of the screen door snagged her attention. Every muscle in her body stiffened, her breath caught.

Colin, his eyes still focused on her own, hadn't heard the sound. His back to the house, he couldn't see the tiny figure standing in the doorway. But Nikki could, and she saw the whole of her universe start to crumble around her even before Carly spoke.

"Mommy?"

Chapter 2

Colin stared at the child in the doorway while his mind desperately scrambled for a plausible explanation to the scene that was unfolding in front of him. He couldn't breathe, he couldn't think. He felt as though he'd just been blindsided at center ice, and he was helpless to do anything as the world spun out of control around him.

"Mommy, I had a bad dream."

He saw Nikki move toward the child, smooth a trembling hand over the little girl's tousled blond hair.

Mommy.

Whatever he'd expected when he'd returned to Fairweather, he hadn't expected this.

Nikki had a child.

He shook his head. He couldn't believe it. He didn't want to believe it. But the relationship between the woman and the child was obvious, and triggered a multitude of other questions in his mind. Whose? When? And most heart wrenching of all—how could she have betrayed him in such a way?

Nikki didn't spare him a glance as she crouched down beside the little girl. "What did you dream about, sweetie?"

"I don't 'member." Her bottom lip quivered. "I just woke up an' I was scared."

"It's okay," Nikki soothed, wrapping her arms around the child. "Mommy's here."

It's been five years. A lot of things have changed in that time.

Her words echoed in his mind. Obviously a lot of things had changed, more than he ever would have expected.

Nikki had told him she'd never married again, and he'd mistakenly assumed that meant she'd never loved anyone else. The existence of this child proved otherwise.

The pain of knowing she'd been with another man, loved another man, was like losing her all over again. It was a betrayal of everything they'd shared, of all that they'd meant to each other.

You were the one who wanted the divorce.

Dammit, he hadn't wanted the divorce. He hadn't wanted anything more than he'd wanted to be with Nikki. But his career had made that impossible, and he couldn't bear to see how much their separation hurt her.

So he'd said goodbye; he'd walked away. And she'd found someone else. As he stared at the blond head nestled against Nikki's shoulder, the realization simply shattered him.

Somehow sensing his perusal, the little girl turned. The initial shock of hearing her call Nikki "Mommy" was nothing compared to the impact he felt when the child looked at him through eyes that were the mirror image of his own.

Colin grasped the railing behind him for support as a whole new wave of emotions washed over him. The most overwhelming, and the most unexpected, of them all was joy. Pure, unadulterated joy filled his heart as he stood face-to-face with his child.

His child.

There was absolutely no doubt in his mind, not the slightest hint of uncertainty in his soul. This beautiful little girl was his daughter.

She, however, obviously had no clue about his identity, because she turned to her mother and demanded, "Who's that?"

Nikki looked from the child to him, her teeth sinking into the soft fullness of her bottom lip in what he recognized as one of her nervous gestures.

Colin waited for her response, silently daring her to deny what was now so painfully clear.

"This is—" she cleared her throat "—Uncle Shaun's brother."

Uncle Shaun's brother.

The words were a double-edged sword—slashing through him with the denial of his parental relationship and the startling realization that his brother had been privy to the deception.

The child tipped her head back to study him more carefully. "Are you my uncle, too?"

At another time, Colin might have been impressed by her deductive reasoning. Now, however, he was too stunned to speak.

"Colin, can you, uh, just give me a minute? Please."

He heard the plea in Nikki's voice, the desperation.

He wanted an explanation and he wanted it *now*. After more than five years, he didn't want to wait another minute. The numbing shock that had settled over him earlier had been supplanted by bubbling hot fury. He wanted to shout, to rage, to demand. He wanted to shake Nikki, as he'd been shaken by this revelation. But he knew that the worst thing he could do right now was confront his ex-wife about her lies in front of their daughter.

He nodded tersely.

"Come on, Carly." Nikki put an arm around the child's shoulders, pointedly ignoring her earlier and still unanswered question. "Mommy will tuck you back into bed."

Colin watched them walk back into the house together, unable to tear his attention away from his little girl.

He'd never given much thought to the possibility of having a family. But faced with the indisputable evidence that he had a child, there was no doubt in his mind that he needed a chance to be her father. A real father—the kind of dad he'd never had.

Unfortunately, he wasn't sure he'd get that chance. He was on the run, hiding out from someone who wanted him dead. How could he pursue any kind of relationship under those circumstances? How could he expect to be her father when he might have to leave town without a moment's notice?

This time he did hear the creak of the screen door, and he turned as Nikki came back out onto the porch. Tension radiated from her slight frame in waves, but she faced him defiantly. "Her name's Carly. She's four-and-a-half years old."

"She's mine," Colin said.

It was a statement rather than a question, but Nikki nodded anyway. "Yes."

"Why didn't you tell me?"

She looked at him, her eyes filled with sadness and regret, but she didn't respond.

He slammed his fist against the wooden post, and Nikki flinched. "Dammit, Nicole. Why didn't you tell me?"

He caught a glimpse of tears in her eyes before she averted her gaze.

"I think I deserve some answers." Colin's voice practically vibrated with tightly restrained anger. He didn't care. He figured he was well within his rights to be angry, and the fury was more tolerable than the fear that had followed him across the country and easier to deal with than the inexplicable longing to take her in his arms.

Nikki drew in a deep breath, nodded stiffly again.

"It's been more than five years, and you never said a word. Not one-single-goddamned word."

A single tear slipped onto her cheek, trailed slowly downward. "I'm sorry. I never wanted you to find out this way."

"Or maybe you never wanted me to find out at all."

She shook her head. "I wanted to tell you—I was going to tell you."

"You're five years too late."

"No." She managed to glare at him through her tears. "*You're* five years too late."

There was just enough truth in her words to infuriate him. "Don't try to blame this on me. You should have told me as soon as you found out you were pregnant. Or didn't you know at the time that it was my baby?"

He wouldn't have thought it was possible, but her already pasty cheeks paled further.

"There was never any doubt," she said softly. "But if that's what you think of me, then maybe it doesn't matter what I did or should have done."

"Maybe it doesn't," he agreed callously.

Nikki managed to hold back the tears until Colin had stormed off. She listened to the slam of the car door, the gunning of the engine, the squeal of tires as he pulled out of the driveway. She waited until his vehicle was out of sight before she went back inside, then she tiptoed up the stairs to check on her sleeping daughter.

She brushed the soft curls back from her forehead, then pressed a gentle kiss to one rosy cheek. Carly didn't even stir. Whatever unpleasant dreams had disturbed her slumber earlier had obviously been banished, and she slept deeply now, contentedly.

Of course, she had no idea that her life as she'd always known it was about to change.

Or maybe not.

Colin had been shocked to learn that he had a child; he was furious that Nikki hadn't told him about their daughter. But maybe, once he had some time to think about it, he'd decide there was no place in his life for a child. Maybe this revelation would inspire him to leave town as unexpectedly as he'd returned—forever this time.

Nikki sighed, knowing in her heart that although Colin's disappearance might be the easiest solution to the problem, it wasn't what she wanted for Carly. Despite the emotional scene on her porch, she was glad he'd come back, relieved he finally knew.

There had been so many times over the years when she'd wanted to call him, so many times she'd wanted to share her feelings—her hopes and dreams for their child, so many milestones she'd wished he'd been a part of.

She slipped from the room, closing the door softly behind her, and for the first time since Carly was born, she allowed herself to cry for everything she and Colin had lost. Everything their daughter had missed out on by not having her daddy in her life.

When Arden came home a short while later, Nikki's tears were finally spent. Her cousin dropped a copy of the *Fairweather Gazette* on the coffee table before sitting beside Nikki on the sofa. "I guess I don't have to ask if you've seen him."

Nikki shook her head.

"What happened?"

"He showed up here and Carly decided to make an impromptu appearance."

Arden winced. "Not the best way he could have found out."

''I know. And I know you warned me.'' For the past five years, Arden had been trying to convince Nikki to contact Colin, to tell him about their daughter.

But she still believed she'd done the right thing.

Colin had made it clear that he'd wanted out of their marriage, he'd wanted to sever the ties that held them together. And a marriage was little more than a piece of paper, a legal institution. A child was flesh and blood, a lifelong responsibility. The last thing Nikki had wanted was to use their baby to try to hold on to him. She'd loved him too much to settle for less than his love in return.

''Are you okay?'' Arden asked gently.

She grabbed another tissue and wiped her nose. ''This morning, I thought I was in complete control of my life. Then Colin showed up and turned everything upside down.''

''You had to know he'd come back sometime.''

''I used to think he would,'' she admitted. ''For the first year after he'd gone, every time there was a knock at the door, I was half hopeful, half afraid, that it might be Colin. Then, as the weeks turned into months, and the months into years, I was less certain. With each passing day it became more apparent that he wasn't coming back, until I'd convinced myself that he never would.''

''But now he has.''

''Yeah.''

''How did he react?''

''He thought…'' She hesitated, surprised by how much it hurt to replay Colin's words in her mind. She could still see the accusation in his eyes, hear the challenge in his voice. ''He thought I hadn't told him because I didn't know if he was the father.''

''Oh, Nic.'' Arden wrapped her arms around her. ''You know he didn't mean that. He's hurting, and he lashed out. It's a normal reaction.''

She gave a short, bitter laugh. "There's nothing normal about this situation."

"Give him some time."

Somehow Nikki didn't think any amount of time would diffuse Colin's anger. "You have no idea how much I wish I could turn the clock back."

"He had to be told."

"I know." She sighed regretfully. "I just wish I'd actually told him."

Colin drove for a long time after he'd left Nikki's house. Although a part of him wished he'd stayed and forced Nikki to give him the answers he needed, another part—maybe the more rational part—recognized that his emotions were running too close to the surface to be able to have a civilized conversation with her right now.

Instead, he got into his car and drove. It was a habit he'd acquired as a teenager—a way of venting steam after one or another blowup with his father—and one that was usually successful in helping him gain perspective on an issue.

Unfortunately, he was sure he could drive all the way to Texas and back and still not gain any perspective in this matter. He tried to sort out his feelings, but everything was so jumbled up inside he didn't know where to begin. He didn't know how he felt, how he was supposed to feel in the face of Nikki's revelation. Mostly, he felt betrayed by the only woman he'd ever trusted with his heart.

It's been five years. A lot has changed in that time.

Her words echoed in his mind again. She was right. A lot of things had changed—Nikki had changed. The woman he'd known, the woman he'd loved, would never have kept such a secret from him.

He still couldn't believe she'd had a child and never told him about it.

Not just *a* child.

Their child.

He winced, remembering the absolute devastation he'd seen in Nikki's eyes when he'd challenged her about not knowing the child's paternity. He'd had no right to make such an accusation, no reason to believe she'd ever been unfaithful.

But how could she have done this to him?

Okay, so maybe he wasn't completely innocent in this scenario. Maybe he shouldn't have walked away from their marriage. But dammit, it wasn't as if he'd known she was pregnant.

He scrubbed a hand over his face. Well, now he knew. But he didn't know what he was going to do about it.

He didn't know anything about being a father. His own had hardly been a shining example. Richard McIver had dedicated his life to the legal profession and nothing—not the woman he'd married nor the two sons she'd given him—had ever competed with his career. He'd been absent more than he'd been home, and disinterested in his children when he was around.

Now, with no warm-up, no practice, no preparation, Colin was a father.

Oh, hell. Who was he kidding? He was more of a sperm donor than a father. That was the extent of his involvement in his daughter's life thus far. He knew nothing about her other than her age and her name. He didn't know her birthday, her favorite color, her favorite toys.

And he didn't know what she knew about him. What had Nikki told their daughter about her father? How had she explained his absence to their child? Did Carly hate him for not being around? Or did she understand why he hadn't been part of her life? Did she even want a father, or would his sudden appearance be an unwanted complication?

The unfairness of the situation struck deep. It wasn't

just that he didn't know anything about his child—he'd never been given a chance to know her. Nikki had deliberately and continuously kept the existence of their daughter a secret for almost five years. Even now, because of a disgruntled player and circumstances out of his control, he might not get a chance to stay in Fairweather long enough to know her.

He thought again of the *Gazette* and the possibility—remote though it seemed—that the article could compromise his cover. While a part of him welcomed the opportunity for a showdown with Parnell, a chance to end things once and for all, he wouldn't risk that confrontation occurring where his child could get caught in the crossfire.

Whether by accident or design, as he pondered these issues he found himself driving down Meadowvale Street toward his brother's house—the home in which they'd both lived as children. He and Shaun had been close at one time, but after he and Nikki split up, Colin had resolved to stay as far away from Fairweather and all reminders of his ex-wife as possible.

He knocked at the door, then waited with something close to apprehension for his brother to answer. He hadn't been back since his father's funeral, and he wasn't sure he wanted to be here now.

"My prodigal brother finally returns." Shaun's quick smile took the sting out of his words before he enveloped his brother in a quick hug. "It's good to see you."

"You, too," Colin told him, surprised by the sudden tightness in his throat.

"This family reunion calls for a celebration," Shaun said, leading the way into the kitchen.

"You might not think so once you find out why I'm here."

Shaun took a couple bottles of beer out of the fridge, twisted the cap off one and passed it to his brother, then did the same to his own. "You've seen Nikki," he guessed.

"And my daughter."

"Good."

Whatever reaction he'd expected from his brother, this wasn't it.

"I'm glad she finally told you." Shaun moved toward the living room.

Colin managed a smile as he followed. "That isn't exactly what happened."

"Oh." Shaun propped his feet up on the coffee table— something neither one of them would have dared to do while their father was still living. "What did happen?"

"Nikki and I were having a conversation about something else entirely when Carly walked in."

"Well." Shaun took a pull from his bottle. "That must have been a surprise."

"To say the least," Colin agreed.

"Then you and Nikki argued about it," Shaun guessed.

He nodded.

"And you walked out."

"Yeah," he admitted.

"I can imagine how upset you must have been, but you're going to have to talk to her if you want to work out a schedule for visitation."

"I don't want visitation," Colin said, cringing at the implications of the word.

"What do you want?"

"I don't know," he admitted. He didn't know anything about being a father, but he knew that he wanted to *be* a father—not just someone who passed in and out of his child's life.

His brother shook his head. "That's typical, isn't it?"

"What's that supposed to mean?"

"You never think things through, Colin. I know you're

pissed that Nikki didn't tell you about Carly, but can you blame her?''

"Yes! I had a right to know that she was carrying my child."

"And she had a right to expect that you'd honor the vows you'd made."

"I did honor those vows. I never cheated on Nikki. I never even thought about another woman while we were together."

"You weren't even married a year."

That was true, but what Shaun didn't know was that it had been a long time after the divorce was final before Colin looked at another woman. Even then, it had been part of a conscious effort to forget about Nikki. A futile effort, he realized now. Because he hadn't stopped thinking about her. Dreaming of her. Missing her.

He'd actually looked forward to receiving the final divorce papers, as if those pages could somehow eradicate his feelings for Nikki. Unfortunately, they'd failed to do so. Nothing had helped him get over his ex-wife.

The minute he'd seen Nikki striding across the parking lot, he'd known his feelings hadn't dissolved with their marriage—they'd only been buried. It had taken just one glance to bring them back to the surface, one touch to have them churned up again. And when he'd kissed her, it was as if the five years apart had never happened, as if nothing had changed.

Except that *everything* had changed.

"I understand that you're angry," Shaun relented, "but—"

"I don't think you can understand any of this. *You* didn't just find out that you had a four-and-a-half year-old daughter." Colin slammed his empty bottle down on the table. "Why would she keep something like this from me? Did she really think I would turn my back on my own child?"

"Nikki didn't find out she was pregnant until after you'd told her your marriage was over."

"I still had a right to know."

Shaun sighed. "Why do you think I tried so hard to get you to come back here? Why do you think I made those outrageous demands in the settlement negotiations with your lawyer?"

"Because you were acting on your client's instructions," Colin guessed.

"Nikki didn't want anything from you," Shaun told him. "But I thought—I'd hoped—that you'd come back here and demand to know why she was being unreasonable. Then she would have had to tell you about the baby she was expecting."

Colin shook his head, only now beginning to understand what he'd previously seen as his brother's betrayal. "My lawyer told me not to sign that agreement. But the money didn't matter to me, and I figured it was the least I could do to compensate Nikki for messing up her life." In fact, he would have paid ten times as much in the hope that the financial settlement might assuage his guilt. It hadn't.

"She's never touched a dime of it," Shaun confided. "It all went into a trust account for Carly."

This revelation didn't change the basic facts of the situation; it didn't absolve his brother of culpability. Shaun had been a party to Nikki's deception for the past five years—the two people he'd been closest to had betrayed him.

"How could *you* keep this from me?" he wondered aloud. "How could you not tell me I had a child?"

"It wasn't my place to tell you. And Nikki was my client—"

"I'm your *brother*."

"I couldn't disclose information provided to me in my capacity as legal—"

"Spare me the speech on attorney-client privilege. You haven't billed Nikki for every conversation you've had over the past five years."

Shaun sighed. "I know she wanted to tell you."

Colin raked his hands through his hair again. He'd been back in Fairweather less than forty-eight hours, and already his life bore little resemblance to the one he'd left behind in Texas.

It had been Detective Brock's suggestion that he get away, and Colin had been grateful to do so. He was tired of always looking over his shoulder, always wondering what might be around the next corner. He'd come back to Fairweather for some downtime, to talk to his ex-wife. His plans had been simple.

Now that he was here, it seemed he'd only exchanged one set of complications for another. Nothing was simple anymore.

"What's she like?" he asked after a long pause. Then, to clarify—and to try the name out, "Carly."

His brother smiled. "She has your eyes, and all of the famous McIver charm."

Colin smiled, pleased to know there was something of himself in his daughter.

"Is she…is she happy?"

"She's an incredibly happy and well-adjusted child."

Colin cleared his throat, to ease the sudden tightness. "Maybe she doesn't need a father," he said. "Not a father like me, anyway."

"What does that mean—a father like you?"

He pushed himself up from the chair. "Just that I don't know anything about being a father. I know nothing—less than nothing, even—about kids."

"Most fathers are novices the first time around."

"But…God, I've never even *thought* about having kids."

"Well, you'd better start thinking about it," his brother said practically. "Because you've got one now."

"Did you…" Colin hesitated, almost afraid to finish the question. "Did you tell her not to tell me…about the baby?"

"No." Shaun grinned. "In fact, I advised her to go after you for child support."

Chapter 3

The worst thing about prison, Duncan Parnell decided, was the bed. If the narrow mattress on the steel frame bolted to the concrete floor could even be called a bed. He rolled slowly onto his back and stretched out, concentrating on his breathing as he tried to force his muscles to relax. Perspiration beaded on his forehead as he gritted his teeth against the stabbing pain.

He wished he had some of his pills, just to take the edge off. Even one pill. One pill would at least reduce the agony to a dull ache.

The guard had given him an aspirin, as if that would make a difference. He closed his eyes as the pain struck again, exhaled slowly. It was a good thing he wasn't going to be here very long.

And when he got out, he'd make Jonesy pay for ratting him out. He didn't doubt for a minute that it had been Jonesy who had turned on him.

McIver had picked Jonesy up from Detroit on a mid-season trade. He'd scored seven goals in his first ten games with the Tornadoes, and after Duncan's accident, he'd been moved up to Duncan's line to fill the vacant position. It was supposed to have been a temporary move, just until Duncan was back.

But McIver kept Jonesy in the starting line. As the team neared play-offs, Jonesy was getting at least twice the ice time Duncan got.

He'd made the mistake of shooting off his mouth in The Thirsty Duck one night after their play-off run had ended. Not to Jonesy—he and the pretty boy from Michigan weren't that close. But Jonesy had been there, and Duncan had been furious enough to rant indiscriminately about his intention to make McIver pay.

Jonesy must've figured he'd be guaranteed Duncan's place in the lineup next season if Duncan was behind bars.

And now, because of a few ill-chosen words and the subsequent explosion at McIver's apartment, Duncan was a guest of the local correctional facility on charges of uttering threats. He knew the cops expected to pin the bombing on him. He also knew that they didn't have any evidence against him, nor would they find any. Because he hadn't done it.

If he'd planned to blow McIver away personally, he would have bought a gun and been done with it. He might even have enjoyed it. But no way would he have tried to build a bomb. Hell, he'd known a guy in high school who lost two fingers on one hand because he'd been playing with a firecracker.

Duncan shook his head. It was too much of a risk. His hands were his livelihood, his life. He wasn't as big as some of the guys, he wasn't as quick on his feet as others, but give him the puck and he could skate circles around all of them. He'd been admired for his "fast hands" since he'd started playing junior hockey at fourteen years of age. No way in hell would he risk his biggest asset.

You had to be nuts to play around with explosives.

Which is exactly what he'd told the cop who'd arrested him.

As the excruciating pain in his back eased a little, he smiled up at the bare ceiling. No, he wasn't the type who got his kicks playing with explosives—but he knew someone who was.

And Boomer had been more than happy to take care of Duncan's problem. He didn't worry about being ratted out. Boomer had been in the business more than fifteen years, with only two arrests and no convictions. He was a man who took pride in his work and his reputation, and Duncan trusted him to get the job done. Which was another reason he didn't mind being locked up right now—he'd have an irrefutable alibi when McIver's body was found.

Nikki was up with the sun Saturday morning after a sleepless night. She knew her conversation with Colin the previous evening had barely scratched the surface of the issue, and the next round of conflict was inevitable. So she was almost relieved to find him at her door before nine o'clock.

"Where's Carly?" Colin asked.

"She's spending the day with Arden."

His cool gaze narrowed on her. "I want to see my daughter."

"I wanted to be able to discuss the…situation without being overheard."

Her explanation didn't seem to placate him.

Nikki didn't care. She was only worried about how Colin's sudden appearance would impact Carly's life. And concerned about the void that would be left after his inevitable disappearance again. Because as much as she wanted Colin to have a relationship with Carly, she knew he wouldn't stay in Fairweather. He'd never wanted to before; there was no reason to suspect he would now.

"Do you want some coffee?" The offer was made in an attempt to buy time rather than because she had any real desire to pump more caffeine into her system.

"Fine."

She could tell by the clipped tone that he was still angry. Furious, in fact, and she knew she couldn't blame him for that.

She led the way into the kitchen, then busied herself pouring coffee into two mugs while she sought the words that would explain her actions. She added a splash of cream to his, cream and sugar to her own. The task gave her another precious moment to compose herself, organize her thoughts.

She turned back to the table and handed him the mug. His fingers brushed against hers and her tenuous composition dissolved, her supposedly organized thoughts fled. She chanced a quick glance at Colin, found his eyes locked on hers, felt the heated awareness that simmered between them.

Despite the enormity of the issues unresolved, the basic attraction was still there. Like the glowing embers of a fire, stoked by that simple, accidental contact of their fingers. It was just another distraction she didn't need right now, a complication she couldn't afford.

"I'm still trying to understand what happened, Nicole, why—in all this time—you didn't tell me we had a child."

Whatever excuses she'd used to justify the deception initially, the more time that passed, the harder it became to even consider telling him about their child. And the older Carly got, the more unreal the whole situation seemed. Maybe it would have been easier when Carly was a baby, or even a toddler. But how could she track

him down to tell him that he was a father—to a four-
and-a-half-year-old child?

She'd always fallen back on the excuse that if Colin
had cared about her at all, he would have come back.
She'd clung to that justification, reveled in it. After all,
he'd been the one to walk out on her. But now he was
back, and she'd run out of excuses.

"I wanted to tell you," she admitted.

"Then why didn't you?"

"Because the day I found out that I was pregnant was
the day I got served with divorce papers." The memory
of that day—both the overwhelming joy and the devas-
tating pain—was still vivid in her mind.

"This was payback? Your way of punishing me for
ending our marriage?"

She sighed wearily. "I didn't think of it as punishment,
but maybe it was. At first, anyway. I was hurt and angry,
and I didn't want to have any contact with you."

"You couldn't have got past your hurt and anger for
two minutes at any time in five years to tell me I had a
child?" he demanded.

"I tried to call you."

"When?"

"The first time I held our baby in my arms." Even
now, thinking about that moment made her smile. "I
wanted you to know about her—our beautiful, perfect
little girl."

"And?" he prompted impatiently.

"The number was no longer in service."

Her response didn't even slow down his attack. "Did
you call directory assistance? Did you ask my brother?
Did you make any effort other than that one phone call?"

"No," she admitted.

"Why, Nic?"

"I thought I was protecting Carly."

"How could you possibly use our child to justify your actions?"

Our child.

The words leaped at her, angry, accusing. Reminding Nikki that he had a valid and legitimate claim to the little girl that she'd kept to herself for so many years. It didn't matter that her actions had been well-intentioned, that she'd given Carly all the love and attention and affection any child could need or want. Carly was his child, too, and she'd hurt all of them by denying it.

"What did you think you were protecting her from?" Colin demanded.

Nikki shifted her gaze, tried to keep her own temper in check. But it was hard not to respond in kind to his anger. "From being rejected by her father."

He scowled. "What are you talking about?"

"I'm talking about your damn obsession with hockey." She practically shouted the words at him, relieved to finally speak them aloud. To finally admit the feelings she'd kept bottled up inside her for so long.

"Obsession?" Colin echoed.

"It was all you ever talked about, all you thought about. And I didn't think a child would fit into your plans. A wife certainly hadn't."

"Hockey wasn't an obsession—it was my life."

"I know," she admitted, helpless to prevent the bitterness from entering her voice. "And more important to you than anything else."

"That isn't true."

"Isn't it?"

"Of course not. And we weren't talking about my career, anyway. We were talking about why you kept my daughter from me."

Nikki sighed. "When I first suspected that I was pregnant, I hoped that having a baby would bring us closer again. Then you decided that being married wasn't what you wanted, and the last thing I wanted was for you to come back to me just because I was pregnant.

"I loved you too much to use our baby to hold on to you. I didn't want you to resent me, and our child, for keeping you here when it wasn't where you wanted to be."

She swallowed around the lump in her throat. "And there was a part of me that was afraid it wouldn't be enough to hold you, anyway. That you would still choose your career over your family."

"Did you ever consider a third option—that I might have wanted to be a father to our child?"

Of course she'd considered it. When the doctor had confirmed her pregnancy, she'd fantasized about telling him. In that fantasy, Colin had been ecstatic to learn she was carrying his child. He'd shouted with joy and kissed her breathless. Then he'd taken her away and they'd lived happily ever after in a house full of children.

But the reality was that they'd married without ever talking about children. At the time, she'd been so thrilled to be Colin's wife she hadn't worried about anything else. She'd known she wanted to have his child some day, and she'd taken it for granted that he wanted the same thing.

When she'd finally broached the subject a couple of months later, she'd been both shocked and hurt to hear him say he didn't want a family. But she hadn't pursued the topic, certain he'd change his mind over time.

Being served with a petition for divorce had effectively annihilated that fantasy. Still, she knew now that she'd been wrong to blame him for destroying a dream he couldn't have known about. And after a long minute of agonizing silence, she finally whispered, "I'm sorry."

"Sorry that I found out?"

She shook her head, blinked back tears. "Sorry that I didn't try to tell you sooner. Regardless of what happened between us, you are her father and you had a right to know.''

Colin remained silent.

"I am sorry," she said, surprised at how good it felt to say those words. "I never meant to hurt you or Carly by keeping my pregnancy a secret. And I'm sorry that's what happened."

"So am I."

"What do you want me to do now?" she asked helplessly. "I've apologized. I've tried to make you understand why I made the decisions I did. Okay, so maybe I screwed up. Maybe I should have done things differently. But it's too late to change that now."

When he finally spoke, his tone was ripe with bitterness and accusation. "I don't know if I can ever forgive you for this."

"We both made mistakes," she reminded him. "Can't we just admit that and move on?"

"I don't know how to get past your lies, your deception."

Nikki again felt the sting of tears behind her eyes.

"Does Carly know anything about me?"

"She's only started to ask questions about her dad," Nikki admitted. "I've told her as much as I can without lying to her."

His eyes narrowed. "What have you told her?"

"That he didn't live with us because he worked in Texas."

He seemed to consider her explanation for a long moment.

"It's not a big deal to her," Nikki explained. "A lot of her friends live in single-parent families."

"It's a big deal to me," he said.

"That's not what I meant. I was only trying to explain that she hasn't missed not having a father."

"Does that help you sleep at night—believing she doesn't need a father?"

"I didn't say she didn't need a father," she said wearily. "In a perfect world, every child would have two parents who love her. But this isn't a perfect world, and I've done the best that I can for Carly."

"Then where do I fit in?"

Nikki hesitated, knowing that her response was only going to infuriate him even more. But she'd thought about that question all night, and she was determined to put her daughter's interests first. "I don't want you forcing your way into her life if you don't plan on staying. It would be worse for Carly to find her father and lose him, than never to have a father at all."

"Why is that your decision to make?" Colin challenged.

"Because she's my daughter and I don't want her to be hurt." As soon as the words were out of her mouth, she recognized her mistake. Of course, it was already too late.

"She's *my* daughter, too," he shot back. "And I want to be part of her life. I want her to know who I am."

"You want her to call you 'Daddy'?"

"I am her father," he reminded her.

"You can't expect to show up, after five years, and—"

"I might have shown up sooner," he pointed out coldly, "if I'd known about my child."

"*Might* being the operative word," Nikki shot back.

"In any event," Colin continued, his tone icy, "I don't think you're in any position to put conditions on my relationship with Carly."

"I'm the one who will have to deal with the fallout when you're not around anymore."

"I'm not going anywhere."

"What happens if your contract is renewed in Texas?"

"I'm not going to debate with you about something that might or might not happen," he said.

''She's the one who'll be hurt when you leave town again.''

''Why are you so quick to assume that I'd abandon her?''

Nikki looked away. She was afraid for Carly, but she was also afraid for herself. Colin affected her as no other man ever had, and she couldn't bear to see him walk out on her again. And she knew that he would leave. Sooner or later, Colin *always* left.

''Because you're always looking for something better. And when a situation becomes a little too difficult, you walk away rather than trying to make it work.''

''Are you still talking about Carly?'' he asked. ''Or us?''

Nikki flushed. ''Obviously our history has colored my perceptions, but you can't blame me for wanting to protect Carly.''

''I would never hurt her, Nikki.''

I would never hurt you, Nikki. Yes, she'd heard those words before. She'd even believed them at one time. Not anymore.

''If you really want to be her father, you have to start thinking about what's best for Carly. You need to consider how it will affect her when you walk out of her life as abruptly as you've walked into it.''

''Dammit, Nicole. What do you want from me? What am I supposed to do to prove that I'm committed?''

''I don't know,'' she admitted. ''But you don't get to call yourself her father until you're ready to take the responsibility of being a father.''

''Maybe we should see what a family-court judge says about it.''

The words, once they'd been spoken, surprised Colin as much as they surprised Nikki. He certainly hadn't

come over here this morning with the intention of threatening to take her to court. But he should have expected
the unexpected—nothing had gone according to plan
since he'd walked back into this town.

And although he was tempted to follow through on the
threat, to force Nikki to accept him as part of Carly's life,
he knew he couldn't. Court documents were a matter of
public record, accessible to anyone who cared to look.
Filing a legal claim to his daughter would not only announce his location to the world but potentially endanger
Carly as well.

Despite Detective Brock's phone call last night advis-
ing of Duncan Parnell's arrest, Colin remained wary. Unless and until Parnell signed a confession, he couldn't let
himself believe the threat had passed. He couldn't let his
guard down for a minute, which meant he couldn't sue
for custody of his child.

But Nikki didn't know this, and her face drained of all
color in response to his impulsive statement. "You
wouldn't dare."

"Don't tempt me," he warned.

She blinked back the tears that shimmered in her eyes.
"I'm only trying to do what's best for Carly. Why can't
you see that?"

"How can not knowing her father be best?"

"It has to be better than knowing he didn't care
enough to stick around."

He raked his fingers through his hair. "Dammit, Nikki.
I didn't know you were pregnant."

"And I didn't think you'd care!"

Her outburst, and the depth of her anger, stunned him
into silence for a moment.

"How could you think that?" he asked at last. "How
could you think I'd walk away from my child?"

"I didn't know what to think," Nikki said bluntly.

"But I didn't think the man who'd told me he'd love me forever would serve me with divorce papers ten months after our wedding, either."

"You know why I ended our marriage," Colin said.

"No, I don't. I've listened to all the reasons you've given to justify your decision, but I still don't understand how you could walk out when you supposedly loved me. How could I be sure that you wouldn't walk out on your child, too?"

"Because I wouldn't," he said simply.

He might be a lot of things, but irresponsible wasn't one of them. Having a baby wasn't something they'd planned, but if he'd known she was carrying his child, he would have done everything in his power to make their marriage work.

"You told me you didn't want kids."

He frowned, having only a vague recollection of a conversation in which she'd asked him about children. It had been shortly after their wedding, and he'd been too preoccupied with his new wife and his lost career to think about anything else. He probably had said he didn't want them, certainly not at the time.

"Maybe I did," he agreed. "But there's a huge difference between the theory of a child and the reality of a little girl who is my own flesh and blood."

Which reminded him of another issue that had nagged at the back of his mind since he'd first set eyes on Carly. He'd been stunned, not just by the fact that Nikki had had a child, but by the realization that he'd fathered the child. Because if there was one thing in his life that Colin had always been circumspect about, it was birth control.

He *always* used protection. Even after he and Nikki had been married, he'd kept a supply of condoms in the bedside table. He'd never made love to her without one.

Except…

"When is Carly's birthday?" he asked abruptly.

She showed no hint of surprise at the question. "October sixth."

He did a quick mental calculation, confirmed from her response what he'd only just begun to suspect: their child had been conceived the very last weekend they'd been together. The weekend he'd come home to bury his father.

Nikki nodded, somehow following his thoughts, confirming his conclusion.

That weekend had been hell for Colin. He'd been overwhelmed with grief and guilt, and he'd willingly lost himself in the comfort she'd offered without thought of the consequences—without thought of anything but how much he needed her. He'd taken advantage of her warmth and her compassion and her love, and then he'd walked out on her.

He scrubbed a hand over his face. The separation necessitated by his job had been difficult for both of them, and that weekend he'd finally acknowledged the truth of what his father had been saying—Nikki deserved more than a husband who was gone most of the time. She deserved so much more than he could give her.

He'd ended their marriage not because he didn't want to be with her, but because he wanted her to have the life she deserved. A husband who could be with her, the family she'd always wanted. It had almost killed him to think of her with someone else, but he'd forced himself to walk away, to give her that chance.

At the time, he'd honestly believed he was doing what was best for Nikki. As she'd done what she had for their daughter.

So how could he blame her for keeping her pregnancy a secret when her reasons so closely paralleled his own?

Nikki finally sank down into one of the vacant kitchen chairs, obviously drained by their argument. "I think what's more important than what either one of us did five years ago is what you want to do now.''

"I want to be a father to my daughter.''

Her hesitation spoke volumes, and had his anger rising again.

"For how long?'' she finally asked. "How long are you going to stick around and actually be part of her life?''

He was so damned tired of rehashing the same argument, of feeling guilty for the decisions he'd made. Mostly he hated that he couldn't give her a definitive answer. Because until he knew for certain that the threats against his life were past, he couldn't promise her anything.

"I'm here now,'' was all he said.

Colin left Nikki's house with a lot of issues still unresolved but with a firm date set for him to see Carly: tomorrow.

Nikki and Carly had plans to go to the botanical gardens for a picnic in the afternoon, and Nikki had reluctantly agreed to let him tag along. They were still at odds about the "daddy" versus "uncle" matter, but Colin was so excited about actually spending some time with his daughter, he almost didn't care what she called him.

By the time he got back to his hotel, apprehension was warring with anticipation. He knew nothing about children, less than nothing about his own child. Had he pushed the issue too soon? Had he forced all of them into a situation that none of them was prepared for?

He had to admit, it wouldn't be the first time. When Nikki had agreed to marry him, he'd rushed her to Vegas without fully considering the magnitude of such a step. He'd loved her, but that love hadn't been enough to sustain their marriage.

Was his pursuit of a relationship with his daughter destined to the same fate?

No, he refused to believe it. This was different. This was about his child. He'd already missed the first four-and-a-half years of her life; he refused to miss even one more day.

The ring of his cell phone was a welcome interruption from his disquieting thoughts.

"Hello?"

"Where are you?" came the impatient demand.

He recognized his agent's voice immediately.

"I'm in Fairweather," Colin told him.

"Didn't you hear the news? The police arrested Duncan Parnell."

"Yeah. Detective Brock called me last night."

"Then why the hell are you still in Pennsylvania? Get your butt on a plane and get back here."

"I'm not coming back," Colin said. "Not right now, anyway."

A long, stunned silence followed his announcement. Then Ian finally asked, "Why not?"

He didn't even know where to begin to answer that question. "It's a long story."

"It's a woman, isn't it?" Ian didn't wait for a response. "Dammit, Colin, haven't I always warned you that women are the downfall of men?"

"And you have four ex-wives to prove it," Colin finished for him. "Yeah, you've told me the story."

"Obviously you weren't listening."

"You're my agent, not my personal advisor. And as my agent, I need you to look into a job opportunity for me."

"You're not unemployed yet," Ian reminded him. "The new owners haven't made a decision about your contract."

Colin ignored the protest. "There's a new cable station

launching in Fairweather in September—an all-sports channel—that's looking for on-screen personalities.''

Ian groaned. ''You don't know anything about television.''

''Just get me an interview and a screen test.''

''You're sure about this?''

''Positive.''

For the first time in five years, he knew exactly what he wanted, and he wasn't going to let anything stand in his way of getting it.

Chapter 4

Nikki hung up the phone, wondering why she was surprised that Colin had bailed on their plans at the eleventh hour. And why she felt let down.

"I'm glad I didn't tell Carly he was coming with us," Nikki told Arden.

"He's not?"

"No. 'Something came up,'" she repeated his explanation scornfully.

Arden frowned. "Something that couldn't wait?"

"Apparently not." She wasn't disappointed, she assured herself, she was annoyed. After all, he was the one who'd insisted on spending time with Carly. The only reason she'd agreed was that she felt backed into a corner, his casual threat about taking her to court still looming in her mind.

The biggest irony was that she'd glanced at her calendar this morning and realized it was Father's Day. And she'd actually been pleased that Carly would, for the first time in her life, spend Father's Day with her daddy.

"That doesn't sound like the same man who badgered you into letting him spend the day with Carly," Arden said.

"No," Nikki agreed. "Although it's not the first time he's changed his mind about what he wants." They both knew she was referring to the marriage Colin had ended before their first year anniversary.

"He didn't offer any kind of explanation?"

She shook her head. "No." Not now, and not five years ago, either. "It just doesn't make any sense."

Then again, not a lot about this situation did make sense. She'd once loved Colin with her heart and soul. She'd believed he loved her. Five years later, there was no hint of the tender affection they'd once shared. All that remained were bitterness, remorse and accusations—and a little girl who didn't deserve to be at the center of their battle.

"How am I going to explain any of this to Carly?" she wondered aloud.

"She's four years old," Arden said gently. "She won't require as much explanation as you think."

"She's going to have to be told *something*."

"She'll deal with it," Arden said. "Kids are amazingly resilient."

"She shouldn't have to be resilient," Nikki said. "She shouldn't have her world turned upside down because of the mistakes I've made."

The pitter-patter of footsteps forestalled any further conversation, and Nikki managed a smile as Carly skipped into the room.

"Mommy, I'm hungry."

The familiar refrain transformed the forced smile into a more natural one. "You're always hungry."

"But it's been a really, really long time since breakfast,'' Carly said solemnly. ''And my tummy is hungry for chocate chip cookies.''

''Chocate chip cookies?''

''Uh-huh,'' Carly affirmed, nodding her head for emphasis.

''You know the rule—no choc-o-late—'' Nikki enunciated the word ''—chip cookies before lunch.''

Carly's lower lip jutted out and her deep green eyes—eyes so much like her father's—pleaded. ''But I'm hungry.''

Nikki wrapped her arms around her daughter and pulled her onto her lap. She breathed in baby shampoo and bubble gum. The unique scent of her little girl.

''Are you okay, Mommy?''

''I'm okay.'' Nikki pressed a kiss to Carly's soft cheek. ''I was just missing holding you.''

Carly wriggled to get down. ''Maybe you need a chocate chip cookie, too.''

Nikki laughed as she released her. ''Maybe I do. And we can both have one *after* our picnic.''

Colin had vowed that nothing would interfere with his plan to spend Sunday afternoon with his daughter. A single phone call had proved otherwise.

Four days later, including a day and a half of arduous and circuitous journey, he was finally back at the Courtland Hotel in Fairweather again. He sank down on the bed, wanting nothing more than a few hours of mindless slumber.

He'd barely closed his eyes when his cell phone started to ring. He should have left it in the car. He didn't want to talk to anyone, and he definitely didn't need any more bad news.

But what if it was Nikki?

What if something had happened to Carly?

He grabbed the phone before the third ring.

It wasn't Nikki. It was Detective Brock calling from Texas.

Colin had forgotten that the detective had promised regular updates on the investigation. He assumed that was what this call was about.

"Do you have any new information for me?" he asked.

Brock ignored the question to ask one of his own. "Are you in Maryland?"

A chill snaked through his body. "No."

"Then why are you registered at the Baltimore Courtland Hotel?"

He knew now that this definitely was *not* going to be good news. "You warned me that I might be followed," Colin reminded him. "I checked into the hotel there as a diversionary tactic."

"Smart move," the detective told him. "An IED was discovered in the bed of your hotel room."

IED. It took Colin a minute to remember the acronym: improvised explosive device—a homemade bomb.

He swallowed. "How was it found?"

Brock was silent for a long moment.

"What happened?" Colin demanded.

"Apparently one of the night managers knew the room wasn't really in use and decided it would be the perfect place for a rendezvous with his girlfriend."

Brock hesitated before admitting, "They were both killed."

He closed his eyes as a fresh wave of grief, of guilt, washed over him. He'd just come back from Maria's funeral, and now two more innocent people were dead. A man and a woman with friends and family who would gather to mourn their senseless deaths.

He closed his eyes, picturing all too clearly the grief-stricken faces of Maria's children. Despite their tragedy, they'd been nothing but gracious, thanking him for his generosity as an employer and his consideration in taking the time to attend their mother's funeral.

They didn't blame him for Maria's death. Then again, they didn't know about Parnell's threats. They didn't know that he could have prevented what happened. If only he'd taken the threats seriously, if only he'd gone to the police sooner.

Now it was too late.

Was there any hope of stopping these attacks? Or would it only end with his own funeral?

The police had believed Duncan Parnell was responsible for the explosion in his apartment. Colin was less certain. Despite the threats Parnell had made, Colin didn't believe the kid had either the guts or the know-how to build a bomb.

"I guess this blows your theory about Parnell," Colin said. After all, Parnell could hardly have planted a bomb in Baltimore when he was in prison in Texas.

"Not necessarily," Brock said. "The evidence suggests that both of these jobs were done by a professional."

"Are you suggesting he put out a hit on me?" Colin almost laughed.

"All it takes is money and connections. And a complete lack of regard for human life."

He no longer felt like laughing. "What should I do now?"

"Exactly what you've been doing—keeping a low profile. And you might want to notify your local police about the situation."

"Do you think I'm in danger here?" He couldn't bear to think that someone had followed him to Fairweather, that he might unwittingly have brought the threat into Nikki and Carly's backyard.

"I'd say it's unlikely. The fact that our bomber struck

in Baltimore suggests he doesn't know where you really are."

Colin wished he could be assured of keeping it that way.

Nikki was on her way home from the grocery store Thursday night when she found herself driving by the Courtland Hotel. It wasn't the usual route she would have taken, and she wouldn't admit—even to herself—that she'd wanted to see if Colin's rental car was in the lot. It was.

Impulsively she pulled into one of the visitor's parking spaces. She found her way to room 1028 and knocked, waiting for what seemed like an eternity before he appeared at the door.

His weary eyes widened. "Nicole."

She was startled by his appearance. His hair was disheveled, his jaw shadowed with at least two days' growth of beard, and there were dark circles under his eyes. "Can I come in?"

He stepped back to allow her entry.

She glanced around, found that his "room" was really a suite, complete with kitchen, dining area and living room. The sofa and chairs in the sitting area were covered in an ornately textured slate-blue fabric that she guessed was silk. The tables were gleaming chrome and smoked glass.

It was a huge step up from her worn upholstery and stained carpet, and yet another reminder of the different worlds in which they lived.

"Do you want something to drink?" Colin asked.

She shook her head. "I didn't come here for a drink. I came here for an explanation."

"That's what I figured." But he didn't say anything more for a long minute as he found a bottle of beer in the minibar and twisted off the cap.

Nikki watched his movements, fascinated by the

strength and grace of those strong hands. As a player, his most notable skills had been speed and good hands. She remembered that those assets carried over to the bedroom. He'd moved fast enough to get her there, but he'd sure known how to take his time once he'd had her clothes off. And those hands weren't just good, they were phenomenal.

She shook off the thought. She was here for a specific reason, and it wasn't to reminisce about their sexual past. She dropped her purse on one of the end tables. "I want to know why you changed your mind about spending Sunday afternoon with Carly."

"I didn't change my mind."

"That's right," she said scornfully. "Something came up."

He tipped the bottle to his lips and drank deeply.

"Was that 'something' blond, brunette, or redhead?"

He set his bottle down carefully. "Is that what you think—that I blew off my daughter for an hour of personal pleasure?"

She refused to be swayed by his injured tone. "It's the only explanation I could come up with for your abrupt phone call."

"It wasn't something I wanted to talk about on the phone." He scrubbed a hand over his face. "Hell, it's not something I want to talk about now."

"What's not?"

"I couldn't make it to the picnic on Sunday because I had to go back to Texas."

Texas. It wasn't at all the response she'd expected, yet maybe it should have been. "You couldn't even spend four consecutive days in this town without needing a trip to the big city?"

"I didn't go back for kicks," he told her. "I went to a funeral."

She was duly chastised. "Oh."

"Nothing else would have made me break those plans," he told her.

His response had completely deflated her anger. "If you'd told me someone had died, I would have understood."

"I wanted to tell you in person."

She felt compelled to ask, even though she wasn't sure she wanted to know, "Who was it?"

"Maria Vasquez," he told her.

A woman. She swallowed. "Were you…very close…to her?"

"She was my cleaning lady for the past four years."

"Oh," she said again, strangely relieved by his response.

He took a deep breath, staring off into the distance. "Remember the explosion in my apartment—the one that you heard about on the news?"

She nodded.

"Maria was there at the time. She died from injuries sustained in blast."

Nikki's whole body went cold.

She'd assumed—obviously incorrectly—that the explosion had been a minor incident. The realization that someone had been killed—that Colin could have been killed—stunned her.

She looked at him, saw the guilt and regret in his eyes. He was clearly torn up about this woman's death, and she was giving him grief about canceling an afternoon picnic.

"I'm sorry, Colin."

And then, because it seemed like the most natural thing in the world to do, she crossed the room and put her arms around him. She couldn't deny him the comfort he so obviously needed.

"Me, too." He pulled her closer.

She didn't resist, accepting that she needed this as

much as he did. She needed to feel the warmth of his body, the beat of his heart, to prove to herself that he was okay.

She closed her eyes and held on to him, just for a minute.

"It should have been me," he said.

She pulled back just far enough to look at him. "It was an accident, Colin. There's nothing—"

"No," he interrupted, dropping his arms and turning away from her. "It wasn't an accident. Someone was trying to kill me."

The icy feeling returned. "What are you talking about?"

"It was a bomb." He delivered the news coolly, almost dispassionately.

"Who? Why?" The questions swirled through her brain.

"The cops arrested one of my former players. They think he wanted revenge because I cut him from the team."

She shook her head, refusing to believe it. "That's crazy. Lots of players get cut every year without trying to kill their coaches."

"This one has other issues."

"What kind of issues?"

"He was in a bad car accident that caused him to miss several weeks in the middle of the season and he started taking pills to combat the pain."

"And you refused to play him." She knew that as much as Colin liked to win, he wouldn't sacrifice a player's well-being to do so.

He nodded. "He blames me for ruining his career."

"And you can't help wondering if he's right," she guessed.

"I can't help wondering if I shouldn't have handled

the situation differently. If I had, maybe Maria Vasquez would still be alive.''

''It isn't your fault, Colin.''

But she could tell he wasn't convinced, and she didn't know what to say or do to persuade him.

Despite their history, or maybe because of it, the thought of losing Colin forever created an emptiness in the very depths of her soul. An emptiness that she knew no one else could ever fill. He was her first lover, her husband, the father of her child—and as such, there was a bond between them that could never be broken.

''That's the real reason I came back to Fairweather.''

She'd suspected there was more to his return than the explanation he'd given, and she wanted to be angry at his deception. But she was only relieved that he had come home, that he'd been given a chance to know about his daughter.

''The reasons don't matter,'' she said softly, surprising both of them with her easy acceptance. She laid her hand against his cheek, the stubble of his beard rough against her palm. ''What matters is that you're alive, and you're here now.''

Because her gaze was locked with his, she saw the change in his deep green eyes. She saw despair slowly give way to acceptance, acceptance gradually yield to awareness.

Then his lips were on hers, and the kiss sent shock waves reverberating through her entire system. Hot and deep and pulsing. From the top of her head to the tips of her toes and everywhere in between, she burned with desire, ached with need.

She closed her eyes and lifted her arms around his neck, her heart pounding wildly in her chest. His tongue traced the softness of her lips, and they parted instinctively in response. He swept inside her mouth, tasting of

beer and heat and passion, and the intoxicating combi-
nation of flavors made her head spin.

Oh God. She should have known that coming here was
a mistake. And yet, there was a part of her that wanted
this. Needed this. But letting her hormones overrule her
head wouldn't be fair to either of them when there was
no future for them. Not so long as the deceptions of their
past continued to loom between them.

Then his hands were on her, his fingertips skimming
down her ribs, brushing against the sides of her breasts,
and the surge of desire through her veins crowded out
guilt and reason. When his thumb brushed over her nip-
ple, she couldn't think about their past—his abandonment
or her dishonesty. She couldn't think about anything but
the here and now. And then she couldn't think at all.

"I want you, Nicole." He whispered the words against
her lips. "I need you."

She knew she should refuse. She couldn't let this happen. It had already gone too far; she'd be crazy to let it
go any further. But when she opened her mouth to respond, she said, "Yes."

He kissed her again, the pressure of his lips on hers
more intense now, more urgent. Nikki responded to his
demands, met them with her own. She didn't want a seduction. She didn't need to be coaxed or persuaded. She
wanted Colin, and the fulfillment only he could give her.

She hadn't realized he'd found the zipper at the back
of her dress until she felt him unfasten her bra with a
quick, practiced move. His fingers skimmed over her
shoulders, sliding the straps of her bra and her dress down
her arms. Then he tore his mouth from hers and trailed
hot, hungry kisses along the column of her throat, over
her collarbone, down to the slope of her breast. Her head
fell back in surrender, her breathing already fast and unsteady, her muscles quivering.

This was what had been missing from her life.

Excitement.

Anticipation.

Desire.

Wondrous, glorious desire.

He pushed the dress over her hips, the fabric whispering softly as it pooled at her feet. His hands skimmed lower, over the curve of her buttocks.

"You're so beautiful, Nicole."

She exhaled slowly, her nervousness alleviated somewhat by the obvious appreciation in his voice.

"Even more beautiful than I remembered," he told her.

Still self-conscious about her seminaked state, Nikki decided to level the playing field. She tugged his shirt out of his pants, her fingers unsteady as they worked the buttons.

She already knew this was a mistake. From the first time he'd kissed her, she'd known that no other man could ever make her feel the way Colin did. But she was beyond caring. She would take what he was offering and worry about the consequences later.

She pushed the shirt off his shoulders, ran her palms over the hard, muscular planes of his chest. His skin was hot beneath her hands and she could feel his heart beating a furious tattoo beneath his ribs. This proof of his desire aroused her, emboldened her. She nipped at his throat, flicked her tongue over his earlobe. Colin groaned and pulled her closer to kiss her again.

She buried her fingers in his hair, held his mouth to hers. Their tongues danced, mated. She could feel the evidence of his arousal, and the throbbing response between her own thighs.

He lifted her into his arms easily and carried her the short distance to the bedroom. They fell together on top of the bed, a tangle of limbs and needs.

He tore his mouth from hers and lowered his head to

her breast. He ravished the tender flesh with his lips and teeth and tongue until Nikki could hardly breathe. He seemed to be touching her everywhere at once, his fingers and his lips gliding, stroking, teasing, until she was quaking with need. She arched toward him, urging him to hurry, but he continued at the same torturously slow pace, driving her closer and closer to the culmination of her own pleasure. Her hands roamed restlessly over his back, tracing the strong muscles through the heated dampness of his skin.

"Colin...please." She was all but begging, but she didn't care. She only knew that she'd never needed anyone as much as she needed him, right here, right now.

He pulled away from her and started to shed his briefs, then swore.

She sat up, automatically tugging at the edge of the bedspread to cover her breasts. "What's wrong?"

He scrubbed his hand over his face and laughed, but the sound was without humor. "I wasn't prepared for this to happen."

He was talking about birth control.

The realization jolted her back to reality. Even when they'd been married, he'd been almost fanatical about protection. The one time—the only time—they'd ever made love without any barrier, she'd conceived their daughter.

He kissed her—a brief, hot kiss full of passion and promise. "Just give me a minute to go downstairs and—"

"No." Nikki shook her head and slid off the bed. She moved quickly to the sitting area, picked up her dress from the floor and slipped it over her head.

"Nic."

She started at the sound of his voice right behind her, again when his hand settled on her shoulder.

"Please don't go."

She didn't turn—she was too embarrassed to look at him. Or maybe she was too afraid that if she looked at him, her already weakened resolve would completely crumble. Instead, she kept her back to him and zipped up her dress. She took another few seconds to straighten her skirt and strengthen her determination, then she finally faced him. "This was a mistake, Colin."

He shook his head. "The mistake is in pretending it didn't mean anything."

"It didn't," she said. "It was just the heat of the moment, and the moment has passed."

But even she knew it was a lie. Because if the heat of the moment had passed, why was she still burning up inside?

Colin knew he could prove her wrong. All he had to do was take her in his arms and kiss her again, and the heat of the moment that she'd so easily disregarded would be upon them again.

Nicole was running scared, and they both knew it. Hell, the intensity of the passion that had flared between them surprised him, too. Even after more than five years apart, he hadn't forgotten anything about her. Not the sweetness of her scent, the silkiness of her skin, or the passion of her touch.

The one thing he had forgotten, the single fact that was only now becoming clear, was how empty his life had been without her in it.

Unfortunately, he knew that she'd been right to step back. There was too much at stake to lose themselves in the passion of the moment, too much still unresolved between them. And, as Detective Brock's phone call had so painfully reminded him, there was too much that was out of his control.

"I have to get back," she said, not meeting his eyes.

"I'll call you…to make arrangements to see Carly."

She nodded, then moved quickly to the door.

Colin let her go. There was no point in pushing her to acknowledge something neither of them was ready for.

He'd hurt her once, and it was understandable that she'd be wary. But he was afraid, too—of the feelings she stirred inside him, of the emotions he'd never experienced with any other woman, of the vulnerability he'd never wanted to know again. Coming back to Fairweather had forced him to face his past—the only woman he'd ever loved, and the child he'd never known.

Would things have been different if he'd known about Nikki's pregnancy?

That was the question she'd thrown in his face. He wanted to be able to say yes, loudly and unequivocally. But he wasn't so certain. Five years ago, his life had been in turmoil. He'd been given a second chance at a career that had once mattered to him more than anything. What he hadn't realized, until it was too late, was that it hadn't mattered to him as much as Nikki did. He loved the game, all the pressures and excitement, but he loved her more.

He'd made a choice.

The wrong choice.

He hadn't come back to Fairweather to change the past. He'd needed to see her again, but he hadn't expected the attraction between them to be as strong, as volatile, as he remembered. He hadn't expected the desire that hit him so hard, so fast. He hadn't expected to need her still.

And he hadn't expected that she would betray him.

Nikki had been right about one thing. He *was* angry. What she couldn't know was that at least some of that anger was directed at himself, because he knew it was his decision to end their marriage that had cost him the woman he'd loved and the opportunity to share in the first five years of his daughter's life. And although he was back now, even he didn't know for how long. If Detective Brock was right, if Parnell had hired someone to kill him, then the threat was far from over.

Chapter 5

The sound of another knock at the door offered a reprieve from these disturbing thoughts.

This time, when he opened the door and found his brother on the other side, he wasn't at all surprised. Although the large cardboard box Shaun carried was a puzzle. Colin decided to ignore the carton for the moment.

"Was that Nikki I just saw leaving?"

Colin nodded.

Shaun set the box down on the coffee table. "How did things go?"

"Not quite as I'd expected," Colin said.

His brother frowned at the cryptic remark. "Have you made arrangements to see Carly?"

"Not yet," he admitted, unaware of the smile playing at the corners of his mouth. "We got distracted with other things."

Shaun shook his head. "Nikki is the one who will end up hurting when you walk out again."

The argument was close enough to everything Nikki

had been saying about his relationship with Carly to annoy him. "Why is everyone so convinced that I won't stay?"

"Will you?" Shaun challenged.

His anger deflated quickly, and he sank down onto the sofa. "I don't know."

The truth was he'd never intended his visit to Fairweather to be anything other than temporary. And while finding out about Carly made him want to stay, there were other factors to consider. Not the least of which were the questions and concerns raised by Detective Brock's recent phone call.

He'd hoped Parnell's quest for revenge had been satisfied by the bombing in Texas, but the loss of two more lives in Maryland suggested otherwise. Until Colin knew for certain that the danger was past, he couldn't promise to stay. He wouldn't stay if his presence could endanger Nikki and Carly.

"I do know that I want to get to know my daughter," he said.

"But?" Shaun prompted.

Colin shouldn't have been surprised that his brother could read him so well. Still, it wasn't easy to voice what was on his mind. "But…what if she hates me?"

"She's not going to hate you."

"How do you know?"

"Because I know her."

Although he knew it wasn't intentional, Shaun's response put Colin firmly back in his place—on the outside of the cozy little family scene Nikki had created. For the four-and-a-half years of her existence, the only family Carly had known were her mother and Shaun and Arden. Now Colin was back in town and demanding to be part of his little girl's life, and for the first time, he thought he understood some of Nikki's reluctance to let him in.

The understanding, however, did nothing to lessen his resolve.

"She thinks I'm her uncle, too," Colin told his brother. "And I'm thinking it might be easier to let her believe that."

"She needs her father," Shaun said.

"But…" The single word was all he managed, as a lifetime of doubts and insecurities jumbled together in his mind.

"What?"

Colin shook his head. "I've never really been good at anything. Except hockey. And I even managed to blow that."

"How can you blame yourself for the injury that ended your career?"

"If I'd gone to college, I might have had something to fall back on."

"Ah." There was a wealth of understanding in that single syllable. "I never thought you paid too much attention to anything the judge said."

"I tried not to," Colin admitted, "but it's hard to block out something that you hear so many times."

Shaun nodded. "I found something in the attic that I thought might interest you."

"What?"

His brother pointed to the box Colin had almost forgotten was there. Now his curiosity was piqued. "What is it?"

"Open it."

He pushed to his feet, an odd sense of expectation raising goose bumps on his flesh. He pulled the dusty box to the edge of the table and folded back the top flaps to reveal an array of carelessly packed trophies. He couldn't imagine where his brother had found them. He'd thought all the mementos from his hockey career were in storage in Texas.

His fingers wrapped around the gold-colored figurine atop an imitation marble pillar. He pulled it from the box, only then realizing that the figure depicted was a goaltender. Colin frowned and glanced down at the engraved brass plate at the base of the trophy.

Richard McIver—Fairweather Falcons

Colin was stunned. "The judge played hockey?"

"He didn't just play. He was an all-star." Shaun reached into the box and withdrew an old scrapbook. He opened the cover carefully. The pages of the book were brittle and yellowed with age. "These clippings date back to his first year playing Select."

Colin took the book. He didn't recognize the child in the picture, but the caption said it was Richie McIver, goalie for the Fairweather Falcons.

"Richie?" His lips curved. "Who would ever have guessed that His Honor Richard McIver was once a little boy called Richie?"

"I was as surprised as you are," Shaun admitted.

"I can't believe he kept all these things," Colin said. He felt as if he was trespassing, but he couldn't stop thumbing through the pages, desperate for some insight into the man who'd been his father. A man he'd barely known.

He pushed the book aside. "If he played, why couldn't he understand how much it meant to me? Why didn't he show any interest?"

"I think he did understand. Too well." Shaun reached past him to flip to the end of the scrapbook. "I think he was afraid of how much you loved the game."

Colin stared at the headlines.

Falcons Goaltender Out for Play-Offs.

He skimmed farther.

Richard McIver, the Falcons starting goaltender and their most promising draft prospect, will miss the rest of the postseason as a result of an unfortunate accident in last night's close contest against the Madison Mustangs. McIver, a highly touted prospect for the upcoming NHL draft, suffered a broken arm when one of his own teammates fell on top of him as McIver scrambled to cover a loose puck at the side of the net. The Falcons won the game and will advance to the semi-finals, but McIver won't be behind them.

Colin didn't want to feel any empathy or grief for Richard McIver, but the surge of emotion was instinctive, inescapable.

"Why…" He cleared his throat. "Why didn't he ever tell us about this?"

"I don't know."

As much as Colin wished he'd known, he wasn't surprised that the judge hadn't shared this part of his past with his sons. There wasn't much that he had shared. "I always thought he and I had nothing in common. I envied you so much—the bond you shared with him."

"And I envied that you were so independent. You always did your own thing, without seeming to need or want his approval."

Colin had wanted his father's approval desperately, he'd just refused to admit it. "I wished I'd known about this before he died. Now it's too little too late."

Shaun nodded. "He should have told you a long time ago. But that doesn't mean you have to make the same mistake."

"What are you talking about?"

"You and Nikki."

"How does this—" he gestured to the array of mementos "—relate to my situation with Nikki?"

"It's about regrets," Shaun said. "About finding out

the truth too late to change things. It's not too late for you and Nikki. Talk to her. Work things out.''

''Why do you care whether Nikki and I work things out?''

''Because I care about both of you. And Carly.''

Colin packed his father's trophies back into the box. ''I'm so afraid of failing her.''

It was hard to admit his fear aloud, but he knew he needed to talk about his concerns. He needed to know that he wasn't going to screw up Carly's life by wanting to be a part of it.

''Failing who—Nikki or Carly?''

''Both.''

''Why do you think you would?''

''Because I've never been good at relationships. Any kind of relationships.''

''Do they matter to you?''

''Yes.''

''Then you'll make it work,'' Shaun said confidently.

Colin sighed. ''I already screwed up with Nikki once.'' He sank down on the sofa, propped his feet on the coffee table.

''You both made mistakes.''

''What if I'm more like him—the judge—than I thought? Nikki once said I had the same dedication to my career that he did.''

''I don't think that was a criticism. She admired that you didn't give up when you were told you couldn't play hockey anymore. She was so proud of you when you got the offer to coach in Texas.''

Colin remembered. Just as he remembered that it was Nikki's support and encouragement that convinced him to take the chance on a new job. He wasn't sure he could have done it without her. And yet, when he'd made it— when he finally got where he wanted to be—he'd turned his back on the woman who'd believed in him.

"I don't want to be like the judge," he said fervently. "I don't want to neglect my family for my career."

"Then don't."

Colin wasn't convinced that it was that simple, especially after Nikki's comment about his obsession with hockey. He'd often referred to his father's job as the same thing, and he'd wondered if he would have been better off without a father than with one who showed no interest in him.

Even now, knowing why his father was so opposed to his choice of career, he couldn't forgive that indifference. And he wondered if that was why Nikki had thought he wouldn't be interested in their child.

Well, as soon as he confirmed that Nikki and Carly weren't in any danger because of his presence, he was going to prove otherwise.

On Saturday, needing a reprieve from her uncertain thoughts and chaotic emotions, Nikki allowed herself to be persuaded to spend the afternoon with Carly and Arden at Shaun's house.

An avid swimmer, Carly was thrilled to be able to spend the day at Uncle Shaun's pool, and she was already unbuckling her seat belt as Nikki pulled into the driveway behind Shaun's Lexus. As if he'd been watching for their arrival, Shaun came around the side of the house, dressed in a pair of tan cargo shorts and a plain white T-shirt.

"Uncle Shaun!" Carly launched herself into his arms.

He scooped her up and swung her over his head. "How's my favorite girl?"

"Good."

"And how are my other favorite girls?" Shaun asked, turning to smile at Nikki and Arden.

"Ready to relax and unwind," Arden answered for both of them.

"The pool's open." He set Carly back on her feet.

"Can I go swimming?" Carly asked her mother.

"If Auntie Arden goes with you," Nikki told her, removing the cooler from her trunk.

Carly latched on to Arden's hand, tugging her toward the backyard.

Shaun took the cooler from Nikki as she followed him into the house and began transferring items into the fridge.

"Have you seen Colin lately?"

Not since the night she'd almost made love with him—which wasn't a detail she planned to share with his brother. "No," she said instead.

"Are you still mad that he canceled his plans to see Carly last weekend?"

"No." She closed the refrigerator door. "I know why he had to go back to Texas. I just wish…"

"That he'd stayed in Texas?" Shaun prompted.

She smiled ruefully. "Yeah."

"I never thought you were a coward, Nic."

"I never had so much to lose." And although Colin hadn't said anything else about taking her to court, she couldn't forget the veiled threat. Forced to acknowledge the possibility that he could sue for custody, that she could lose her daughter, she thought she finally understood how Colin must have felt to have missed out on the first five years of her life.

"Talk to him," Shaun suggested. "Work something out—for Carly's sake, if not for your own."

She knew he was right, she just didn't know if she could see Colin again without thinking about what had almost happened in his hotel room. Without wishing that things had ended differently.

"Nic?" Shaun prompted.

She felt her cheeks flush. "I'll talk to him."

He smiled as a car door slammed. "There's no time like the present."

Nikki stiffened.

Arden and Carly came into the kitchen through the patio doors off the deck just as Colin entered from the front hallway.

"I need my floaties…" Carly's words trailed off when she spotted Colin. Her little brow furrowed as she tilted her head to study him.

Nikki chanced a quick look at Colin, noted the tension in the set of his shoulders, the muscle that flexed in his jaw, the mixture of uncertainty and hesitant joy in his eyes as he looked at the child he now knew was his daughter.

Then Carly smiled. "You're Uncle Colin."

Colin's Adam's apple bobbed as he swallowed, then he crouched down so that he was at eye level with her. "You can call me Uncle Colin," he agreed.

Nikki exhaled slowly. She didn't know why she'd been granted this reprieve, but she was too grateful to question it.

"Okay," Carly replied, accepting this new member into her family without further question. "Are you going to come swimming with me, Uncle Colin?"

"I'm sure he'll come out in a little while," Arden said. "He has some things to talk about with your mom first."

"I'll go to the pool with you," Shaun offered.

"'Kay," Carly agreed readily. Then, remembering why she'd come into the house in the first place, she said, "I need my floaties, Mommy."

"They're right here." Nikki pulled the inflatable armbands out of the large canvas bag she'd tossed onto the counter.

"They need to be blowed up," Carly told her.

"I'll blow them up," Arden offered. "Outside."

Nikki smiled her thanks. She could barely force the oxygen in and out of her lungs, never mind fill Carly's floaties with air.

Then Carly and Arden and Shaun were gone, leaving Nikki in the kitchen with Colin and a whole lot of tension.

"I didn't know you were going to be here today," she said, after a long moment of awkward silence.

"I asked Shaun not to tell you," he admitted.

"Why?"

"Because after the other night, I didn't think you'd come if you knew."

She wasn't sure how to respond to his statement, this direct reference to the encounter she'd been trying so hard to forget.

"I tried calling you yesterday," he said.

"I was out."

"Obviously." He went to the refrigerator and grabbed a can of soda. "Do you want one?"

She shook her head.

"You didn't return my call."

"It was late by the time I got in and—"

"And you were avoiding me."

"Maybe." Damn, she was going to have to talk about it. If she wanted them to get past it, she had to deal with it. She huffed out a breath. "I know that what happened the other night is a separate issue from your relationship with Carly. It's a non-issue, really, but—"

"Nic?" he interrupted.

"What?"

"You're babbling again."

She looked away. "I'm sorry. I should have returned your call, and I am willing to discuss visitation with you—if that's what you still want."

"I have a better idea," Colin said abruptly.

Nikki leaned her back against the counter and folded her arms across her chest. "What is it?"

He was silent for a long moment, as if already having second thoughts about his better idea.

"I understand you have a downstairs apartment at your house that you were renting to a college student."

"Yes," Nikki agreed hesitantly, suspecting that she wouldn't like what he was going to say.

"And it's vacant now," he continued.

"No," she said quickly.

He frowned. "Arden told me it was."

"It is," she admitted. The student who'd rented the space for the past four years had recently graduated and moved back to her hometown. The rental income from the basement had gone a long way to helping pay the mortgage, but Nikki was undecided about whether she wanted another tenant in her home. She definitely did *not* want her ex-husband living there. "But you can't stay there."

"Why not?"

"Why would you want to?" she countered. "It's a tiny apartment with the barest essentials. No room service or maid service. It's nothing like a Courtland Hotel."

"But if I stayed there, I'd be able to spend time with Carly. I could get to know her, give her a chance to get to know me."

"On Monday Carly will be starting day camp for the summer," Nikki told him.

"Cancel it," Colin said simply.

"I'm not going to cancel it. She's been going to camp for the past two years. It's a good program, and Carly loves it."

"Do you understand the meaning of the word 'compromise', Nicole?"

She flushed.

"Those are my terms," he told her. "I think they're infinitely reasonable. I'll pay rent for the apartment and save you the cost of camp. All you have to do is let me spend time with my daughter."

Nikki blew out an impatient breath. Of course it

sounded reasonable, but it was patently *un*reasonable. How could Colin expect her to let him take up residence in her house—never mind that it was the basement? How could he expect her to hand over her daughter into his care when he had absolutely no experience with children?

Okay, so maybe that wasn't fair. After all, she'd had no experience with children prior to becoming a mother, and she didn't pretend giving birth to Carly had somehow made her an expert. But she wasn't concerned about being fair. She was concerned about Carly.

"It's really not much of an apartment," she said.

"I don't need much," Colin told her. "I'll even agree to remain 'Uncle Colin' for now."

"Why?"

He shrugged. "Because I've done a lot of thinking about what you said, and I agree that it might be confusing to Carly to suddenly be confronted by the father she never knew."

She exhaled a silent sigh of relief.

"I'm trying to do what's best for Carly," Colin said. "I don't want my presence to upset her life, but I'm going to be part of it. Whether you like it or not, you're going to have to get used to it."

"I want you and Carly to spend time together," Nikki said. "I just don't think you need to live at my house to do it."

"I want her to get used to having me around."

Nikki bit back a sigh. She couldn't dispute his point, but she didn't want Carly to start *expecting* him to be around. She didn't want her daughter's heart to be broken when he went back to Texas. But she didn't share these feelings. She already felt as though she'd said too much. Revealed too much. Not just about her concerns about their daughter, but about her own feelings.

He closed the distance between them. "Why are you opposed to the idea?"

"Maybe I'm concerned about your reasons for coming back to Fairweather in the first place—about that fact that someone was trying to kill you."

"Detective Brock has assured me that I'm safe here."

"And I'm just supposed to accept that? I'm supposed to ignore the potential danger to Carly and—"

"Dammit, Nicole. Do you think I would have suggested this arrangement if there was even a possibility it would put you and Carly at risk?"

"I don't know," she said.

"Well, I wouldn't."

"Maybe not intentionally," she allowed. "But—"

"Not at all," he interrupted.

Nikki sighed. She knew in her heart that he spoke the truth. Just as she knew that she was only looking for excuses to keep him at a distance.

"So what are you really afraid of, Nicole?"

"I don't know," she admitted. But she was afraid. And Shaun's spacious kitchen suddenly seemed much too small for both of them. She took a half step to the side, and he took half a step closer.

"Maybe you're wondering if living in such close proximity will rekindle the passion between us."

She gave a shaky laugh. "I don't think that's something we need to worry about."

"Have you already forgotten what happened in my room Thursday night?"

"What *almost* happened," Nikki said, wishing she could forget about it. Wishing the memory didn't keep her awake at night. "And it was a mistake."

"Maybe it was," he allowed. "But I still want you."

She hated that his words caused a tingle of pleasure to dance along her spine. It was ridiculous, this attraction between them. How could she even contemplate the pleasures of physical union with this man when her daughter's future was at stake? "You can't…"

He smiled thinly. "Oh, believe me, I can. And I do. Whether or not I'm willing to do anything about those feelings has yet to be decided."

The cocky self-assurance in his tone was enough to put her back up. "Whether or not you're willing, if you think I'm going to fall into bed with you again, you can forget it."

"I think the physical side of our relationship is the most honest thing we have between us. Regardless of how we might feel about each other, the attraction is real. Undeniable."

She lifted her chin a notch, prepared to deny it. But the banked heat in the depths of his green eyes made her falter.

"Go ahead," Colin said silkily. "Tell me it's not true. Give me a reason to prove you wrong."

She was trapped. Saying nothing would be a silent affirmation of his statement; a denial was pretty much an invitation for his kiss.

"I—"

That was as far as she got before his mouth covered hers. She put her hands against his chest, intending to push him away. Instead her fingers curled into the soft fabric of his shirt, holding on, as she kissed him back.

She felt his arms wrap around her, holding her close to the heat of his body. His lips were hard, punishing. But Nikki understood. There was a lot of emotion between them: hurt, anger, resentment. And floating just beneath the surface: passion.

About that, Colin was right. There had always been passion between them.

Her hands slid over his shoulders to clasp behind his neck. Her fingers tangled in the silky strands of his hair.

This was the passion he'd talked about. Real and undeniable. But passion without affection was cold, empty, and Nikki's heart balked even as her body embraced him.

Suddenly the tenor of the kiss changed. The bruising pressure of his mouth lessened, the tension in his body eased, and she realized there was tenderness underlying the passion. Sweet and gently persuasive.

Her heart sighed. This was the man she remembered. The man she'd fallen in love with so many years ago.

The man she wished she could hold on to forever.

Or at least for a few more minutes.

It was Colin who ended the kiss, easing his lips from hers slowly. Her eyelids flickered open, and her gaze locked with his. It wasn't until he brushed his thumbs over the trails of tears on her cheeks that she realized she was crying.

"There's something about you," Colin said hoarsely. "Even when I know I'm going to regret it, I can't stop myself from wanting to be near you, wanting to be with you. Wanting you."

She wasn't sure what, if any, response she was supposed to make to that kind of blunt statement. She wasn't sure how she felt to hear that he regretted kissing her while her lips still tingled from his touch.

"I'm already starting to think that moving in to your house will be a mistake," he admitted, "but it's the best solution I can think of right now."

Even as she nodded her reluctant acceptance of his terms, Nikki knew in her heart that it was a very bad idea.

Chapter 6

"I still think this is a bad idea," Nikki said, standing at the window as Colin unloaded his suitcases from the trunk of his rental car. "A very bad idea."

"It's a compromise," Arden reminded her. "A necessary one."

Nikki sighed. "I know, but that doesn't mean I have to like it."

"Well, if you're right, he'll last about two weeks in the downstairs apartment. If you're wrong—"

"I'm not wrong," Nikki interrupted.

But, oh, how she wished she was. Carly had taken to Colin immediately, not even batting an eye when her mother told her that she wouldn't be going to day camp this summer but would be staying home with 'Uncle Colin.' In fact, Carly had been thrilled.

Which only worried Nikki more. She didn't believe Colin would be content to spend his days as a baby-sitter. Soon he'd move on, and it would be better if Carly never knew that he was her father.

"Then just hold tight for a couple of weeks," Arden said. "Besides, he might surprise you."

"Maybe." But Nikki doubted it. "I just hope I'll be able to get Carly into day camp when he bails out."

"I don't want to go to day camp," Carly protested loudly. "I want to stay with Uncle Colin."

Nikki started, wondering how much of the conversation her daughter had overhead. She'd thought Carly was upstairs playing. "What are you doing down here?" she asked.

"It was time for Emma's nap," Carly told her, referring to her newest favorite doll—a gift from "Uncle Colin."

"How about you?" Nikki asked. "Is it time for your nap, too?"

"I'm too big for a nap," Carly said.

"Usually that's true," her mother allowed. "But you were up early this morning."

"'Cause I was 'cited 'bout Uncle Colin moving in."

Nikki, too, had been awake early. Because she was apprehensive about the same thing.

"Can Uncle Shaun move in, too?" Carly asked.

Nikki smiled. "I don't think so. Uncle Shaun has his own house."

"Why doesn't Uncle Colin have a house?"

"He did have a house in Texas," Nikki explained. Well, he had an apartment, but she figured the distinction was irrelevant to Carly. "Because that's where he used to live."

"Like my daddy," Carly said.

Nikki had forgotten that she'd shared this information with her daughter, but Carly was always surprising her with the tiniest details she retained about her father. Nikki couldn't help feeling guilty for her continued deception regarding Colin's relationship to Carly. Even though she believed it was for the best, at least for now.

"Can I go see if Uncle Colin needs any help?" Carly asked.

"It's probably better if you stay out of the way until he's had a chance to unpack and get settled."

"Please, Mommy."

Nikki sighed. This was one of the reasons she hadn't wanted Colin living downstairs. But since that decision had been taken out of her hands, all she could do was adjust. Or pretend to adjust, anyway.

"Okay," she agreed. "We'll go outside and see if Uncle Colin needs any help."

Colin was just closing the trunk of his car when she and Carly stepped onto the porch. He smiled warmly at his daughter. "Hey, Squirt. Whatcha up to?"

Carly giggled at the nickname. "I wanna help you move in."

"I don't have a lot of stuff," he told her.

"That's good," Nikki said dryly. "Because there's not a lot of room."

"I'm sure it's more than adequate," he said, before turning his attention back to Carly. "Have you seen my place?"

She nodded. "Becca—the lady who lived there before—used to baby-sit me sometimes."

"Then maybe you can show me around," Colin said. "Make sure I don't get lost."

Carly giggled again. "You won't get lost." But she looked to her mother for permission.

Nikki hesitated a fraction of a second, wrestling with the urge to sweep her daughter into her arms to protect her forever and knowing in her heart that it wasn't possible. She nodded. "You can go with Uncle Colin."

Carly didn't even cast a backward glance at her mother as she placed her small hand in Colin's much larger one. Nikki felt a pang in her heart as she watched them stroll around to the back of the house together.

Did it bother her, she wondered, that Carly had taken to Colin so quickly? Or was it that there seemed to be no place in their cozy little circle for her?

There was enough room, Colin decided, looking around the apartment that would be his home for the immediate future. What there wasn't a lot of was stuff. The rooms were sparsely furnished: a single bed, tall dresser and night table in the bedroom; a sofa, television set, desk and chair in the living area; a small table and two chairs in the kitchen. Still, the apartment had a comfortable, cozy feel to it.

"Do you like it, Uncle Colin?" Carly looked up at him worriedly.

He'd stayed in his share of five-star hotels and ocean-view resorts, but no luxury accommodation in the tropics could compete with the presence of his little girl. "It's perfect."

She grinned. "Can I watch TV?"

He started to nod automatically, then wondered if Nikki was one of those parents who disapproved of television. "Does your mom let you watch TV?"

She nodded, her wide-eyed solemnity tugging at his heart even as his brain warned that he was being scammed.

"All the time," she told him.

Colin chuckled. "Okay," he said, making a mental note to verify Nikki's television policy later.

She picked up the remote and punched the power button. Her easy familiarity with the device reassuring him a little, Colin turned his attention to unpacking. He'd just begun transferring his clothes from the suitcase to the dresser when his cell phone rang. Moving to the doorway of the bedroom to keep an eye on his daughter, he connected the call.

"I just wanted to give you the heads-up before you hear it on the news," Detective Brock told him.

"Hear what?" he asked warily.

"Duncan Parnell has escaped from police custody."

"What? How?"

"He was being transported to a psychiatric facility for assessment earlier today when the van he was riding in was involved in a collision. Somehow, Parnell got out.

"It's only been a few hours," Brock continued. "And we've put out a state-wide APB so I don't think he'll get too far, but I thought you should know."

"I appreciate it," he said.

"I'll be in touch as soon as we have any more information."

Colin nodded and hung up the phone.

He returned to the task of unpacking and wondered how to break the news to Nikki. He knew he should tell her about Brock's call, just as he knew he couldn't do it. She'd been reluctant to let him move in here to begin with; this news would be the ammunition she needed to terminate the arrangement. And any hope he had of building a relationship with his daughter would be destroyed.

He would never have suggested staying here if he'd thought his presence would put Nikki and Carly at risk. But he'd believed, after the second bombing in Baltimore, that he was safe here. There was no reason to believe any different just because Parnell was on the run.

All he could do now was wait, trust the police to track down Parnell and pray that he hadn't made the biggest mistake of his life in moving into his ex-wife's house.

Almost two hours passed before there was a knock on the back door. Arden had gone out for a meeting with a client, and Nikki had spent most of those two hours pacing and worrying. It was ridiculous. She knew it, but she couldn't stop it.

When she opened the door for Colin and Carly, the sense of relief was almost overwhelming. She checked the urge to pull her daughter into her arms and merely smiled.

"All the unpacking done?" she asked.

Carly nodded. "An' we watched *Cosmic Cat.*"

"I wasn't sure if that old television still worked," Nikki said.

"It gets about three channels," Colin said. "But I had to take Carly's word for it that the cat is orange. He looked kind of green to me."

"She," Nikki corrected automatically.

"She—who?"

"The cat," Nikki explained. "Cosmic Cat is a girl." Not that it mattered, in the large scheme of things, but she didn't know what else to say. She didn't know how to make casual conversation when there was so much tension between them, when just the memory of his kiss was enough to make her blood heat, her nerves jolt.

"Oh." Colin's response indicated that he was having just as much trouble with the whole conversation thing as she was.

"Uncle Colin said we can have pizza for dinner," Carly said, breaking the awkward silence that had fallen.

"*If* it's okay with your mom," he reminded her.

"Oh. Yeah," Carly agreed. "Is it, Mommy? Can we have pizza?"

Nikki had already put chicken in the oven, but she knew Carly would rather have pizza. She wasn't going to be the villain by denying the request, but at the first opportunity she was going to talk to Colin about this. She couldn't afford to compete with him if he started trying to buy Carly's affections with her favorite foods and gifts, and it wouldn't be healthy for their daughter, either.

"Yes, you can have pizza," she agreed.

"Goody!"

"What do you like on your pizza, Squirt?" Colin asked.

"Pep'roni and mushrooms."

"Nic? Do you still like pineapple and olives?"

"Yes, but don't—"

"I'm making an effort here," Colin interrupted her. "I thought it would be nice if we could all sit down and have dinner together."

She pushed aside the instinctive hesitation. If he was willing to make an effort, she could at least do the same. "Okay."

Twenty minutes later she sat with a slice of pizza in front of her, wondering how it had happened that she was sharing a meal with her ex-husband and their daughter. Carly was chattering away about anything and everything, for which Nikki was grateful. She still didn't know what to say to Colin, how to bridge the awkwardness between them—or even if she wanted to. The adversity was easier to deal with than the attraction.

And she *was* still attracted to him. The kiss they'd shared in Shaun's kitchen when she'd agreed to this crazy living arrangement proved it. Just as the fact that she'd agreed to this crazy living arrangement proved that his kiss had completely short-circuited her brain.

Neither of them had said a word about that kiss, but the knowledge of it was there—hanging between them like a web. Waiting to ensnare them again.

"Nic?"

She started. "Sorry?"

"I asked if your pizza was okay. You've barely touched it."

"Oh." She picked up the slice. "Yeah, it's fine."

"Do you want some of mine, Mommy? It has mushrooms."

"No, thanks," Nikki said quickly.

"Your mom doesn't like fungus," Colin told Carly, his voice lowered to a conspiratorial whisper.

"What's fungus?" Carly whispered back.

"It's another word for mushrooms," he explained.

"Just tell her they're mushrooms," she suggested, still whispering. "Maybe then she'll like them."

Colin grinned at the child's logic. "I think she'd still know they're fungus."

Carly considered, then nodded. "Just like I know caulifwower isn't white broccli. But that's what Mommy tells me to get me to eat it."

"Do you like broccoli?" Colin asked.

Carly nodded. "But not caulifwower."

"What does your mom say when you don't eat your cauliflower?"

"She says I'm just like my daddy. And that I can't have any chocate-chip cookies until I eat all my vegables."

Nikki's attention was focused on her half-eaten slice of pizza, but she could feel Colin's head rivet in her direction in response to Carly's explanation.

"You must really like chocolate-chip cookies," he said after a long pause.

Carly nodded. "Sometimes I even help Mommy make them."

"Do you like them enough to eat all your cauliflower?"

Carly cast a quick glance across the table at her mother, then shook her head and mumbled something.

"What was that?" Colin asked.

"She said that Arden eats her cauliflower," Nikki told him.

Carly's mouth dropped open in surprise; Colin chuckled.

The warm, rich sound of his laughter stirred something inside Nikki. Something that didn't want to be stirred.

"If you come for dinner, you could eat my cauli-fwower," Carly whispered to Colin.

Colin grinned at her. "I don't like cauliflower, either."

Carly sighed. "Then Auntie Arden will have to eat yours, too."

After they'd finished eating and the leftover pizza had been put away, Colin knew he should be heading back to his new—and empty—apartment. But he wasn't anxious to go. He'd enjoyed the time he'd spent with his daughter, and with Nikki, too. The tension between them had seemed to ease a little over dinner, although he knew it was still there. Maybe it always would be.

"Okay, Carly. Time to get ready for bed," Nikki said.

"Can Uncle Colin give me my bath?" Carly asked.

The absolute panic must have shown on his face because Nikki laughed.

"Ever bathed a four-year-old?" she asked him.

He shook his head. "Before yesterday, I hadn't spent ten minutes with a four-year-old."

"I'm four and a half," Carly said indignantly.

"And you need a bath," Nikki told her.

Carly looked up at him again, her deep green eyes pleading.

"Your mom probably wants me to go home so that she can get you ready for bed," Colin said, providing Nikki with a gracious out.

"Maybe Uncle Colin can watch you have your bath," she suggested. "Then he'll be able to make an informed decision the next time you ask for his help."

Surprised by the offer, Colin nodded. "If you're sure you don't mind my staying a little longer."

Nikki shrugged, as if his decision didn't matter to her one way or the other, and turned to go upstairs to the bathroom.

The bath routine seemed simple enough, except that

Carly liked to make big waves in the water with her array of plastic fish and whales and turtles. By the time Nikki plucked her out of the tub and wrapped her in a thick, terry towel, there was more water on the floor and him and Nikki than there was left in the tub.

Nikki rubbed the towel over Carly briskly, sprinkled her front and back with baby powder, and dressed her in a pair of pajamas with Cosmic Cat on them. Then Carly crawled into bed where a stuffed Cosmic Cat—her favorite toy, or so Shaun had told him—was waiting by her pillow. Beside Cosmic Cat was Emma, the doll he'd bought for her. A pretty little doll with soft blond hair and green eyes like his daughter.

Carly got a big hug and a kiss from her mom, then looked at him expectantly. "Kiss, Uncle Colin."

He smiled and bent over the bed, wondering why it was so easy and natural for her to give and receive affection. Grateful that it was, because he'd quickly learned that there was no feeling in the world like holding his little girl in his arms.

"Night, Squirt."

"Night," she said, her eyelids already closing.

Colin followed Nikki out of the room, watched as she folded the towel she'd used after Carly's bath and hung it to dry.

"I should get out of your hair now," he said.

"If you're not in a hurry, we could take a few minutes to discuss my schedule and your plans with Carly for the week," Nikki offered.

"Okay." Was it reluctance to go back to an empty apartment that caused him to leap at her invitation, an unwillingness to be alone with his thoughts of Duncan Parnell and homemade bombs, or a desire to spend more time with Nikki?

"Do you want a cup of coffee?" Nikki asked.

"Sure," Colin agreed, feeling a little chilled from the

dampness of his clothes against his skin. Damp? He leaned over the kitchen sink to wring the water out of his sleeve.

"I warned you it was an experience." Nikki's lips twitched as she watched him roll back the sodden cuffs of his sweatshirt.

"That you did," he agreed. Anything else he might have said stuck in his suddenly dry throat when his eyes dipped to the front of her blouse. Her white, very wet, blouse.

Apparently unaware of his perusal, Nikki busied herself measuring coffee into the filter.

He tried to divert his focus, really he did. But he could see the lacy pattern of her bra and the outline of her nipples as they strained against the fabric. All he could think about was how completely her breasts filled his palms; how she'd gasp in pleasure when his thumbs stroked the rosy peaks; how she'd writhe beneath him when he suckled. He didn't want to think of those things, but it was a miracle he could think at all with the blood in his head migrating south. And when all he wanted was to get his hands on her.

Oh, this was *not* good.

When he'd first learned about Carly, he'd thought he'd never forgive Nikki for her deception. He still wasn't sure if he did. But he'd been right when he'd told Nikki that the attraction he felt for her existed separate and apart from everything else.

That attraction continued to endure, and it continued to torture him.

"Um…Nic…"

She glanced up as she finished filling the reservoir with water. No doubt she was wondering why he sounded as if he was going to choke on his tongue. "What's wrong?"

"I—you—" He was stumbling over his words like a

toddler in his first pair of skates. "Can you go change your shirt?" He cleared his throat. "Please?"

She glanced down and gasped as she noticed the wet splotches on the front of her blouse. The wet splotches he'd been trying desperately—and unsuccessfully—to tear his gaze away from for the past several minutes.

Her cheeks flooded with color, then she turned and fled from the room. Colin leaned back against the counter, determined to get his raging hormones under control before Nikki returned. Except that he knew she was now in her bedroom, peeling the wet garment from her body, maybe even slipping out of the bra. He could picture, all too clearly, the satiny perfection of her skin.

He groaned in frustration. What the hell was the matter with him? He was thirty-four years old—too old to be getting aroused by the sight of a woman in a wet shirt.

He shook his head, wondering how to get that point across to his erection.

Nikki peeled off the wet blouse and bra, trying not to think about the blatant hunger she'd seen in Colin's eyes, the answering heat that had spread through her veins.

How was it possible to want him so much when he was threatening the stability of her whole world?

She wrenched open the top drawer of her dresser, then remembered that she hadn't brought up the laundry she'd done the previous evening. Which meant she had to either put the wet bra back on or go without one. She opted for the latter, and an oversize dark T-shirt. Now all she had to do was go back downstairs, discuss Carly's schedule over a quick cup of coffee, and get Colin out of her house before she did something to *really* embarrass herself—like jump his bones.

She returned to the kitchen just as the coffee finished brewing. Relieved to have something to do, she busied herself getting cups out of the cupboard.

"I work three full days—Monday, Tuesday, Thursday. Mornings on Wednesday and Friday." She spoke casually, as if she'd never fled from the kitchen.

"What time do you start?" Colin asked, and Nikki exhaled a sigh of relief that he'd so willingly picked up the thread of their conversation.

"My first patient usually comes in for eight o'clock, which means I have to leave here by seven-thirty."

"Seven-thirty," Colin echoed, sounding a little less enthused about the prospect and earning a small smile from Nikki.

"Think of it as early-morning practice," she teased, handing him one of the mugs.

"Is Carly awake at that hour?"

"Only if I have to get her up for school or day camp."

"One more reason not to go to day camp," Colin muttered.

"Just be here at seven-thirty," she said. "You can crash on the sofa until Carly wakes up."

Nikki sipped her coffee, winced. She must have lost count of the scoops as she measured out the grounds because it was strong enough to wake up a corpse. She moved back to the counter to add some more cream, and when she turned around, her shoulder bumped against Colin's chest. The mug slipped out of her hand and bounced on the counter, spilling coffee all over.

She swore under her breath and grabbed a handful of paper towels to mop up the mess. At least the cup hadn't broken. Colin picked up the now-empty mug and set it aside, then put his hands on her shoulders and turned her to face him.

"You're tense." He murmured the words softly, seductively, as his fingers began to knead her tight trapezius muscles.

"I'm fine," she snapped.

"I'll bet I could help you release some of that tension.'' The words were filled with promise and temptation.

''I just need to get some sleep.'' She hadn't slept well since he'd come back to town, and hardly at all last night after agreeing to his ridiculous plan to move in downstairs.

Obviously she'd been right to be apprehensive. He'd been on the premises less than twelve hours and her nerves were already stretched so tight it was a wonder they didn't snap—and fling her right into his arms.

''Sleep isn't quite what I had in mind,'' he said.

She stepped away from him, forcing his hands to drop from her shoulders. ''I have things to do, Colin. I'll see you in the morning.''

He tilted his head, considering. ''Does that usually work?''

Nikki frowned. ''Does what work?''

''The cool attitude, the quick dismissal.''

He moved forward again, slowly, steadily, and slipped his arms around her waist. She felt her breath quicken as her internal temperature rose about twenty degrees.

''I imagine it might be effective on a lot of guys, but I know you, Nic. I know there's heat beneath the ice.''

Heat? If he didn't stop looking at her like that, she was going to spontaneously combust.

''How long do you figure it will be before we end up in bed together again?''

The sheer arrogance of the question should have annoyed her, but his words—and the erotic images they evoked—sent a quick thrill through her. Rather than chance a response, she decided it was safer to ignore the question.

''I give us two weeks, max,'' Colin continued idly. ''Only because I know how stubborn you can be.'' He slid his hands up her back, felt her yield slightly, smiled. ''Maybe ten days.''

How was she supposed to ignore him when he was touching her like that? She tried to push his arms away. "I am *not* going to end up in your bed again," she said through gritted teeth.

Colin nodded. "Your bed would probably be more comfortable," he agreed. "More spacious. Although making love in a single would certainly be cozy."

He slid one knee between hers and drew her steadily closer, until her breasts brushed against his chest. Her nipples tightened instinctively, strained against the fabric of her shirt.

Her breath hitched as his gaze dropped to her mouth, lingered there. Uh-oh. She couldn't let him kiss her again, because if he did, she knew she'd be lost.

"You…uh…really need to go," she said, just a little breathlessly.

Then his lips were on hers and all thoughts of any further protest evaporated. Her mind went completely, blissfully, blank, and there was only Colin. She was vaguely aware of a heart beating, loud and fast, but she wasn't sure if it was his or her own.

This was crazy. It was wrong. He wouldn't stay in town for the long term. He never did. Maybe he'd come back occasionally, now that he knew about Carly, but she couldn't hope for any more than that. He'd already broken her heart once before. She could not—would not—give him that power over her again.

But the demands of her body were much stronger and more insistent than any reservations in her head. And, oh, it felt so good to be in his arms. To be kissed and cuddled as if he really cared about her. As if she mattered.

"Mommy?"

Carly's soft inquiry sounded like an explosion in the silence of the room. Nikki would have leaped out of Colin's arms if he hadn't been holding her so tightly.

He released her slowly, and Nikki turned to her daughter. "Did you need something, honey?"

Carly nodded, yawning. "A drink of water. Please."

Nikki was conscious of Colin's eyes on her as she turned to the cupboard to find a plastic cup, then filled it with cold water from the tap.

"Why were you kissing Uncle Colin?" Carly asked.

Nikki cast a quick glance at Colin, who grinned at her. Damn him! As if she wasn't confused enough about their relationship, now she had to make explanations to her daughter.

Their daughter.

She handed Carly the cup, hoped Colin couldn't see that her hand wasn't quite steady. "Um...well, because that's what grown-ups do sometimes—"

"You don't kiss Uncle Shaun like that," Carly interrupted.

Nikki's face flamed; Colin's grin widened.

"Drink your water," Nikki instructed.

Carly obediently put the cup to her lips and sipped.

"Are you going to kiss again?" Carly asked, her eyes wide as she glanced from her mother to Colin and back again.

"No," Nikki responded.

"Definitely," Colin said at the same time.

Carly smiled, as if she understood.

"You're supposed to be in bed, Carly," Nikki said sternly.

"Why aren't you and Uncle Colin in bed?" Carly asked.

Nikki knew Carly didn't mean *together,* but that was the image that came to mind. Naked, sweaty, their limbs entwined. "Uncle Colin was just going to bed—going home," she amended quickly.

"O—kay." Carly gave a long-suffering sigh, took another sip of water and handed her cup back to her mother.

"Why aren't we in bed?" Colin asked, after Carly had left the room.

"Go home, Colin."

He grinned again. "I'd rather go to bed."

She couldn't prevent the smile that tugged at her lips. He was nothing if not persistent, and it was somewhat flattering to know that he still wanted her. Even though she knew nothing would come of it. She couldn't let it. Having sex with Colin wouldn't solve anything, and it would only make her want things she knew she couldn't have.

"Good night, Colin," she said pointedly.

He touched his lips to hers in a brief but potent kiss. "Sweet dreams, Nicole."

Chapter 7

The melodic chime echoed in the empty room. He rose from his sleeping bag, rolled the kinks out of his shoulders. He hadn't been sleeping; he was too edgy to sleep.

The cutesy tone sounded again, and he reached for the cell. He could have changed the signal, but had opted not to because it had so clearly suited the perky woman from whom he'd liberated the device a couple of weeks earlier. She, too, had been cute, chirpy, and completely oblivious to the fact that he was rifling through her knapsack as he chatted her up on the commuter train.

He wasn't a thief, he was a scientist, but he didn't have a cell phone of his own. He didn't believe in owning anything that could be traced back to him, and he didn't trust that the transmissions were secure. But he appreciated the advantages of technology and took full advantage whenever it suited his purposes. For this assignment, the phone suited his purposes.

He connected the call before the third ring was complete, anticipation shooting through his veins like a potent injection of speed. Of course, he hadn't done drugs since college. His work gave him a thrill that surpassed any artificially induced high. His work also required a clear and focused mind. The slightest distraction or inattention could be deadly.

He put the phone to his ear. "Yeah?"

"You screwed up, Boomer."

He recognized Parnell's voice. It was the call he'd been waiting for, although the words weren't at all what he'd expected. Nor was Boomer—not his real name, of course—pleased with the accusation. "What the hell are you talking about?"

"I'm talking about the fact that you failed to eliminate the target—again." His client seethed with frustration.

"I didn't screw up. I followed through exactly as we discussed." He'd carefully positioned the bomb between the top of the mattress and the headboard. Any weight on the bed would tip the device, causing the mercury to shift and complete the trigger circuit, thus detonating the bomb. And it had worked, dammit. He'd stuck around the hotel long enough to be sure of that fact.

"Except that you set it up in the wrong room."

"It wasn't the wrong room," he insisted. He'd tapped into the hotel computer personally to confirm the details of the reservation.

But the first hint of doubt started to seep into his mind. If he hadn't made a mistake, what was the reason for this phone call? Was Parnell trying to scam him—to hold out on the final payoff? Or did he have a valid reason to claim that the terms of the contract had not been fulfilled?

"The bombing was the lead story on the Baltimore news," Parnell explained. "And the victims were identified as Gordon Reynolds, an assistant manager of the hotel, and Doreen Carr, one of the front desk clerks."

Boomer swore viciously, furiously.

"That was my reaction exactly," his client agreed.

"It was McIver's room," Boomer insisted.

"But McIver wasn't in it."

"Do you think the room was a decoy?"

"It worked, didn't it?"

Damn. "What do you want me to do now?"

"Find him and finish the job."

"How am I supposed to find him?" Boomer demanded. He'd followed McIver's trail from Texas, and that trail had ended in Baltimore.

"That's not my problem, it's yours."

"I need more money."

"You'll get the rest as we agreed—when the job is done."

"I need cash for more supplies," he argued. "It's not like I can pick up C-4 at the local Wal-Mart and charge it to my Visa."

"Why the hell didn't you take what you needed with you?"

"Because the FAA generally frowns upon passengers carrying explosive materials onboard an aircraft."

The client swore, then finally said, "Find McIver, and I'll find a way to wire the money."

"How was your first week?" Nikki asked Colin when she got home from the clinic Friday afternoon. He was sitting on one of the Adirondack chairs in the backyard, his long legs stretched out in front of him, watching Carly jump around the sprinkler he'd set up to combat the early summer heat wave.

Nikki stopped several feet away from him, all too aware of the way her pulse jolted when he was near. She couldn't risk a repeat of what had happened in her kitchen the day he'd moved in.

She'd avoided him as much as possible throughout the week, although Carly was always full of stories about "Uncle Colin" and how they'd spent their time together during the day. As a result of these conversations with her daughter, Nikki had to admit that Colin seemed to be handling his role as caregiver with little difficulty. But she still wasn't convinced he intended to follow through with it for the rest of the summer.

Colin gave a short laugh in response to her question. "Keeping up with Carly isn't easy," he admitted. "But I can't remember when I've had more fun."

She noted the smile that touched the corners of his mouth as he watched their daughter twirl in the water. He seemed as enthralled with Carly as she was with her current activity.

"Then you might be convinced to put in a few extra hours on the job?" Nikki inquired hesitantly.

"When?"

"Tomorrow night. I know it's short notice, and I know it's Saturday night, but I have an obligation that I can't get out of and Arden has other plans and—"

"Okay," Colin said, loudly enough to interrupt her verbal meandering.

"Oh." She hadn't expected him to acquiesce so easily. "Thank you."

"What is the 'obligation'?" he asked.

She ventured closer, perched on the edge of another chair. "The annual fund-raising dinner for the clinic."

"Are you going alone?"

Nikki averted her eyes. "No."

"So I'm going to stay with our daughter while you're out with another man?" he asked.

She picked up the can of ginger ale with the straw in it and took a sip. She grimaced as she swallowed the warm soda. "I'm really out of options," she admitted.

"Then if I were unavailable, you wouldn't be able to go," he mused aloud.

Nikki's eyes narrowed as she set the can back on the

table. "I thought you might like to spend the time with Carly."

"Relax, Nikki. I said I'd stay with her, and I will. What time is your date tomorrow night?"

"Seven-thirty."

"I'll be here," he said.

Colin was at Nikki's door by seven o'clock the following evening. He knew he was early, but he saw no point in hanging around his apartment to watch the minutes tick away. Arden let him inside on her way out, explaining that Nikki was in the shower and Carly was drawing pictures in the living room.

Colin followed the sound of the television and sat down on the sofa beside where his daughter was crouched on the floor. She was focused intently on her task, her brow furrowed with determination, a green marker clutched in her little fist. She added eyes, a nose, and a mouth to the face of a stick figure she'd drawn and carefully put the cap back on the marker before picking up another color.

"Can you make a dog, Uncle Colin?" she asked.

He took the blue marker she offered. "What kind of dog?"

"A blue one," she said.

He smiled. "A big one or a little one?"

She seemed to consider for a minute. "Big. But littler than me."

"Okay." He studied the picture, pointed to the figure she'd just finished drawing. "Is that you?"

Carly nodded.

He put the marker to paper and attempted to sketch something that looked canine in nature.

A few minutes later, Carly giggled at the result. "That looks like a frog."

Colin scowled. It *did* look like a frog.

"Didn't you say frog?" he asked, trying to disguise his lack of artistic talent as a misunderstanding.

She giggled again. "I said *dog*."

"Oh, well." He drew a longer tail. "There you go—now it's a dog."

Carly was still giggling when Nikki came down the stairs. She stopped short when she spotted Colin sitting on the sofa beside their daughter.

"I...didn't realize you were here. Already." She tugged on the lapels of her short silky robe.

Colin let his eyes roam over her boldly, appreciatively. Her hair was secured on top of her head with some kind of clip, but several strands had escaped to frame a face that was scrubbed free of makeup. Her skin was creamy and, he knew from experience, softer than the silk of the robe that covered her from shoulder to mid-thigh. The thin material clung to the gentle swell of her breasts and, as his attention lingered there, her nipples pebbled, straining against the fabric barrier. He lowered his eyes to the belt knotted at her slender waist, lower still to the curve of her hip, the hem of the robe, the smooth, endlessly long legs, and finally to toenails that were painted a vibrant shade of pink.

"Mommy, can you make a dog?"

Carly's request mobilized Nikki, and she moved farther into the room, away from him. "Okay." She flicked a hesitant glance at Colin, then knelt on the carpet beside her daughter.

"Uncle Colin tried, but he doesn't draw good," Carly told her.

"I'm an athlete, not an artist." He felt compelled to point out this fact in his own defense.

Nikki looked down at the drawing, the beginnings of a smile twitching at her lips. "It looks like a frog with a tail."

Carly giggled. "You draw, Mommy. Please."

Nikki took the marker and quickly outlined an animal that at least resembled a dog. Colin didn't mind being shown up. In fact, he wished Carly would ask Nikki to draw something else, because the front of her robe had gaped open as she'd leaned over the table, exposing the soft swell of one rounded breast to his avid gaze.

As if she could read his thoughts, Nikki straightened and tugged on her robe again. She glared at him, and he grinned.

"I'm going to get dressed," she said.

"Need any help?" he asked.

"Just keep Carly out of trouble."

He watched her walk out of the room, enjoying the subtle sway of her hips, the flex of the muscles in her calves, the trailing scent she left behind. The scent that would be forever linked in his mind with Nicole.

"Do you like kissing my mommy?" Carly asked nonchalantly.

She was working on her picture again, drawing a tall stick figure beside the dog Nikki had penned. He cleared his throat, considered an evasive response before settling upon the truth. "Yes, I do."

"I've never seen her kiss anyone before," Carly confided.

"Really?"

"She needs to get out more."

What kind of statement was that for a four-and-a-half-year-old to be making? "Why do you say that?"

"It's what Auntie Arden tells her," she replied matter-of-factly.

"Oh." He ignored the reprimand from his conscience that disapproved of pumping his child for information about her mother.

"She's still in love with my daddy," Carly told him.

He sucked in a breath. "Is that something else Auntie Arden said?"

It was only one question, he promised himself. He wasn't interrogating the child, just filing away the information she willingly provided.

Carly nodded and uncapped a green marker, then began coloring the bottom part of the page.

"What did your mommy say about it?"

Okay, two questions. That still didn't make it an interrogation.

"She said Auntie Arden was wrong. If you like kissing my mommy you could get married and then you could be my daddy."

Colin didn't know if he should be pleased that she'd want him to be her father, or disappointed that it would be so easy for Nikki to find a man—any man—to be a father to his daughter. He was glad that Carly was so obviously well-adjusted. He didn't want her pining away for a father who had never been there for her. But, dammit, he *was* her father, and he didn't want to be replaced by anyone.

Carly drew a yellow circle at the top of the page, then several straight lines extending from the circle.

"There." She capped her marker just as Nikki came back into the room.

"Very nice," Colin said.

Carly skipped out of the room with her picture in hand, and his focus shifted to Nikki. "Very, very nice."

She was wearing a silver-colored sheath dress with skinny straps—and just looking at her had his mouth going dry. The fabric was light and clingy and shimmered as she moved. The neckline was square and the skirt fell almost to her ankles.

Sexy, he thought approvingly—of course, Nikki would look sexy in a tablecloth—but not too revealing. Then she turned around, and his jaw dropped open.

The back of the dress was open to the waist except for

the tiny straps that crossed over her shoulder blades, and the long skirt was slit from the hem up past her knees.

She opened the closet door and rummaged around inside. A few seconds later, she closed the door and turned, one strappy silver-colored sandal with a neck-breaking heel dangling from her fingertips.

He managed to snap his jaw shut. "Is that…" He cleared his throat. "Is that what you're wearing tonight?"

She shot him an annoyed look. "No, this is my shoe-hunting dress. Once I locate the appropriate footwear, I'll change my outfit."

He chose to ignore her sarcasm. "Don't you think it's a little…um…revealing?"

He'd never thought that a woman's back was a particularly sexy part of the body, but Nikki's was truly spectacular. He didn't care to have it bared for the leering eyes of every man at this—whatever this thing was she was going to tonight.

"No."

He scowled, not even sure he remembered the question she was responding to. "Will there be dancing tonight?"

Nikki's brow furrowed. "Probably."

"Slow dancing?"

She stopped on her way back to the stairs and blew out an exasperated breath. "I didn't realize you required a detailed itinerary of the evening's events."

"I didn't realize you'd be wearing something that bares more skin than it covers," he retorted.

She fisted her free hand on her hip, and the action drew the shimmering material tighter across her breasts. "How I dress is none of your business."

"Like hell it isn't," he muttered, shifting uncomfortably on the sofa.

Her other hand still held one shoe, and it was all too easy to imagine her feet tucked into the pair of sexy sandals. Unsatisfied with the five-foot-five-inch frame nature had given her, Nikki had always exhibited a fondness for heels. Colin might have thought everything about her was perfect, but he could still appreciate the way a nice pair of shoes highlighted those shapely legs.

He forced his attention from the sandals back to her dress. "I'm just suggesting that you might want to wear something a little warmer." Something that covered her from neck to ankles. "It's a little chilly tonight."

"It's eighty degrees outside," she reminded him.

"But you'll be inside, where it's air-conditioned." Okay, maybe he should just shut up before he made an even bigger fool of himself.

She stared at him for a long moment before shaking her head dismissively. "Can I go look for my other shoe?"

"Sure. Whatever." If she wasn't going to change her outfit, he was going to have a little chat with her date before they left for the evening.

As Nikki walked away, Colin was left alone to wonder how the hell he'd ever allowed himself to be talked into this situation. He must have been out of his mind to agree to spend the evening with Carly so that Nikki could go out with another man. Temporary insanity was the only plausible explanation.

A few minutes later, Nikki was back and digging through the closet again. She picked up and tossed aside one shoe after the other.

"Haven't you looked in there already?" Colin asked.

"I've looked *everywhere* already. Most places twice," she admitted.

She was still digging through the closet when Carly came back down the stairs, her hands tucked behind her back.

"Mommy?"

"Mommy's kind of busy right now," Nikki said, still from inside the closet.

"I have to tell you something."

Nikki stood up again, sighing as she closed the door, her hands empty. "What is it, honey?"

"I...um...it's about your...shoe," Carly admitted.

Nikki closed her eyes, as if she knew her daughter's words were a prelude of worse things to come. "Where is it?"

Carly chewed on her bottom lip, unconsciously mimicking one of her mother's nervous gestures, and held out the shoe she'd been hiding behind her back.

Colin had to bite down on his own lip to keep from laughing out loud. The shoe in Carly's hand, covered in purple and green marker, no longer bore much resemblance to the one Nikki had been searching for.

"Caroline—Theresa—Gordon."

Caroline. It had been Colin's mother's name, but he'd never realized it was Carly's as well. Nikki hadn't even known his mother, but she'd known how close Colin had been to her, and it meant a lot to him that she'd named their daughter for her.

Looking at his little girl, he saw that the use of her full name was all it took for Carly to appreciate the magnitude of the situation, because her eyes immediately filled with tears. "I'm sorry."

Nikki exhaled audibly and took the shoe from her daughter's hand. "What were you doing with this?"

"I was just playing dress-up," Carly answered.

"You know you're supposed to ask for permission before you use someone else's things," her mother reminded her. "And you don't color or paint or cut or glue anything that isn't yours."

Carly nodded and hung her head.

Colin was impressed that Nikki was able to maintain a level tone and outward calm despite the obvious ruin of her footwear.

"Then why did you draw on mommy's shoes?"

"I wanted shoes like Cosmic Cat," she explained. Her favorite cartoon character habitually wore a pink cape and green-and-purple-spotted shoes.

Nikki sighed again. "Caroline."

The first tears tracked down Carly's cheeks, and Colin felt his heart turn over in his chest. He knew Carly's actions deserved reprimand, but he hated to see the obvious upset on his daughter's face and he longed to take her in his arms and comfort her. Fortunately, before he could give in to the impulse—and annoy Nikki by interfering in the situation—the doorbell rang.

"I'll get it," he offered, grateful for the interruption and looking forward to the opportunity to chat with Nikki's date for the evening.

But when he opened the door, he found his brother standing on the porch.

Chapter 8

"It's not a good time for a visit," Colin said, vaguely wondering why Shaun was dressed in black tie. "Nikki's in the middle of a shoe crisis."

His brother frowned. "I'm not visiting," he said. "I'm here to pick up Nikki."

Now it was Colin's turn to frown.

Shaun was Nikki's date?

Well, that would explain the tux. But it didn't explain the myriad of emotions that coursed through Colin in response to the revelation.

Should he be relieved that Nikki would be with Shaun? Or infuriated that she was wearing that sexy dress for his brother?

"Can I come in?" Shaun asked.

Colin stepped back automatically, his mind reeling. There was no way Nikki was *really* dating Shaun. His ex-wife and his brother? The idea was just too ridiculous.

Shaun would never—

Hell, Nikki was a beautiful woman. Any man would consider himself lucky to be with her.

But Nikki would never—

Well, as Nikki had so clearly stated, he didn't know anything about her. Not anymore.

Maybe Shaun was the type of man she was looking for. He was a successful professional—responsible, reliable. And he'd been there for Nikki over the past five years, which Colin himself had not. The realization didn't sit well with Colin, and although he wanted to be there for Nikki now, he knew he couldn't make any promises. Not until Duncan Parnell was behind bars again and all loose ends were tied up.

A short while later, he stood mutely at the window with Carly as she waved goodbye to her mother and uncle. He watched Shaun put his hand on the small of Nikki's back—his palm against the bare flesh exposed by the low-cut dress—to guide her to his car. There was no awkwardness in the touch, no uncertainty. If this really was a date, it obviously wasn't a first date.

Still, Colin took some comfort in the fact that Nikki had been forced to borrow a pair of low-heeled gray pumps from Arden's closet. While the shoes matched the dress well enough, they weren't the kind of footwear to inspire erotic fantasies. Even as she'd slipped her feet into them, Nikki had grumbled that she wouldn't be able to do much dancing because the shoes didn't fit quite right. Colin had bit back a smile, silently congratulating his daughter on the success of her clever, if unintended, attempt to keep her mother out of the arms of another man.

Hours later, after Carly was sleeping in her bed, Colin continued to puzzle over the situation between his ex-wife and his brother. The idea that they could be romantically involved preoccupied his thoughts to the exclusion of all else. Even his concerns about Parnell and the bombings took a backseat—if only temporarily—to equally unnerving thoughts of a personal relationship between Nikki and Shaun.

When ten o'clock came and went and Nikki still wasn't back, his uneasiness increased. She hadn't said what time he should expect her, and he hadn't thought to ask. She had left her cell-phone number in case of an emergency, but he doubted she'd agree that the thought of his brother holding her too close on the dance floor constituted such an emergency.

He heard the crunch of tires on gravel through the open window and exhaled a sigh of relief. They must have left right after dinner to be home already, which confirmed that the evening was an obligation rather than a date.

He turned up the volume on the television, pretended to be engrossed in the baseball game.

But it wasn't Nikki who came into the house.

It was Arden.

"You're home early," Colin said, ignoring the surge of disappointment.

Arden kicked off her shoes—sensible, low-heeled pumps—and sank into an overstuffed chair, tucking her feet under her. "Not early enough."

"Bad date?"

"The worst," she agreed. "Never, never, never let yourself be talked into going out with someone your single friends assure you is perfectly wonderful," she warned him. "Because the truth of the matter is, if he was that wonderful, he wouldn't be available. And they wouldn't be trying to pawn him off on you."

Colin couldn't help but smile. "Good point."

"Why does everyone think a woman can't be happy unless she has a man in her life, anyway?" she demanded to know.

"I couldn't say," he replied.

"Because I *am* happy," Arden continued. "I'm an independent woman with a fulfilling career and wonderful friends.''

He knew what she was talking about. And because he'd been there, he understood how she could feel lonely and alone despite outward appearances. ''Life sucks, doesn't it?''

She laughed. ''Yeah. Sometimes it really does.'' She pushed herself to her feet. ''I think I'm going to have a glass of wine. Would you like one, or are you ready to head back to your own place?''

''I'll hang around for a while,'' he said casually. He might not have been the man Nikki had spent the evening with, but somehow he'd make sure that he was the man she was thinking about when she went to bed that night.

''Want to see what time she comes home?'' Arden teased, moving over to the dining room cabinet to take out two glasses. She found a bottle of red wine in the cupboard below and deftly uncorked it. ''*If* she comes home.''

Colin's eyes narrowed, but Arden just smiled.

''Does she make a habit of not coming home?'' he asked. He didn't expect that Nikki had been celibate for the past five years, but the thought of her being with some nameless, faceless man was easier to tolerate than that of her with his brother.

Arden passed him a glass of wine. ''Why are you asking? Are you looking for ammunition in case you decide to sue for custody?''

''I'm asking because I can't stand the thought of her being with anyone else,'' he said, surprising both of them with the admission.

''She'll be home,'' she assured him.

''Does Nikki go out…with Shaun…very often?''

She chuckled softly. ''I thought you'd at least *try* to be subtle.''

''Would you just answer the question?''

"They've been out a few times."

"Are they just friends?" he asked. "Or is there something more going on?"

Arden hesitated, and he wished he could withdraw the question. If there was something going on between his ex-wife and his brother, he did not want to know about it.

"They're just friends," she said, "but…sometimes I think he'd like it to be more."

He never should have asked. He should definitely drop the subject. Instead, he said, "What does Nikki want?"

"That, you'll have to ask her."

"She doesn't exactly confide in me these days."

Arden sipped from her glass of wine. "That's not surprising."

"No." He knew he'd made some mistakes. Big mistakes. He would give anything to be able to go back in time and do things over, but since that wasn't possible, he could only hope that Nikki would give him a second chance. And that he would stay alive long enough to take it.

"How are things going with Carly?" Arden asked.

He smiled. "I find myself just watching her sometimes, awed by the realization that I had even a small part in creating such an incredible child."

"She's the best, isn't she?" There was no denying the affection in Arden's voice.

"Yeah, she is."

"She's the reason I suggested this arrangement," she admitted. "Not because you deserved a chance to know your daughter, but because she deserved to know her father."

He ignored the not-so-subtle jibe. "I'm grateful, anyway."

"Don't make me regret it. And—" she hesitated once more "—don't break Nikki's heart again."

Colin's mouth twisted in a wry smile. "She won't let me get that close."

"She's had to be strong," Arden admitted. "But that doesn't mean she's not vulnerable, and I don't want you to take advantage of her feelings for you."

"I would never intentionally hurt her," he said.

"Most damage is done under the guise of good intentions."

Colin's expression sharpened. "Speaking from experience?"

She shrugged off the question. "What do you want from Nikki?"

"I'm not sure," he admitted. "I'm still not even sure why I decided to come back here, except that I knew I had to see her again." Before it was too late. But he kept that thought to himself and sipped his wine. "I was almost hoping that she'd remarried. That she'd have half a dozen kids and three chins."

She laughed. "I guess you were disappointed."

"She has changed," Colin said. "She's even more beautiful than I remembered. More stubborn. More independent.

"I'm sure having Carly had a lot to do with that. I can't even begin to imagine how hard it was for her to go through the pregnancy and childbirth and everything on her own."

"She didn't," Arden said.

"You were there?" Colin asked.

She nodded. "Every minute of sixteen hours of labor."

"I'm glad she wasn't alone," he said softly.

But he still wished he could have been there—to have held her hand, to have heard the first cries of their baby. It was too late to change the past, time to move forward. And he wanted to move forward with Nikki and Carly by his side. Unfortunately, his ex-wife seemed to have different ideas.

Before he could say anything else, the sound of footsteps coming up the front steps drifted through the open window. Arden caught Colin's eye and grinned, but she gamely kept quiet so they could both listen to the murmur of conversation.

Watching through the wide front window, Colin saw Nikki and his brother step onto the porch and into the light that shone over the door.

"Are you sure I can't talk you into extending the evening a little longer?" Shaun's voice was pitched low enough that Colin had to strain to hear his words.

"Thanks, but it's been a long day already and my feet are killing me. I think I'm going to start giving Carly an allowance, just so I can take the cost of the shoes she ruined out of it."

Shaun chuckled.

The initial relief Colin had felt upon realizing that Nikki was home gave way to something else—some darker emotion that he chose not to define—as he listened to their exchange. As he listened to his brother hitting on her.

Then Shaun stepped closer to Nikki, set his hands on her shoulders. It took every ounce of willpower Colin possessed not to barge through the front door and bodily throw his brother off the porch.

"I should be getting in," Nikki said.

"Okay." But Shaun leaned toward her rather than stepping away.

"He's going to kiss her," Colin hissed at Arden.

"That's usually what happens at the end of a date," she replied from behind his shoulder.

Sure enough, that's what happened. He felt a burning surge deep in his stomach as he watched Shaun's head lower until his mouth touched hers. Colin's hands clenched into fists, but lucky for his brother, the kiss was over almost before it had begun.

"Good night, Shaun," Nikki said softly.

Both Colin and Arden scrambled back to their seats as they heard a key turn in the lock of the front door.

"Was that a base hit?" Arden asked, as if she and Colin had been discussing the ball game that still played out on the television.

"Base hit?" Colin was indignant. "He never made it anywhere near first base."

"I don't know," she said, her eyes sparkling with humor. "It looked pretty impressive from here."

He shook his head. "That was strictly minor league."

"As if you could do better," she scoffed.

Colin grinned at the veiled challenge. "You bet I could."

Nikki's keys clinked against the wood as she dropped them on top of the small table in the hallway. She stared at the scene in the living room. Colin and Arden—in the same room together, watching television, sharing a bottle of wine, and discussing baseball?

Arden didn't even like baseball. And Nikki had been sure her cousin wasn't too fond of Colin, either.

Then again, it had been Arden who'd forced her and Colin to talk about the custody issue. And it had been Arden's suggestion that Colin take up temporary residence in the downstairs apartment. But still, Nikki hadn't realized they'd gotten quite so…chummy.

"Oh, hi, Nic." Arden smiled at her.

"How come you're home already?" Nikki asked, stepping out of the borrowed shoes she'd been forced to wear. Her feet practically screamed in relief.

"Don't ask," Arden muttered.

Nikki turned her attention to Colin. "How was Carly?"

"Good. We watched a movie, shared some popcorn."

"Did she go to sleep okay?" Nikki took a seat on the

sofa beside Arden, and began flexing her foot against the leg of the coffee table to work the kinks out.

"After I read her some bedtime story about a big bunny and a little bunny fifty times."

"Rookie." But Arden smiled as she said it. Then she topped up her glass of wine and handed the bottle to Colin. "See you guys tomorrow."

"Do you want a glass of this?" he asked Nikki.

She shook her head. "No, thanks." She needed to keep a clear head around Colin.

He stood up and set the bottle of wine on the coffee table, his glass next to it, then moved to the seat Arden had vacated. "Put your feet up here," he said, gesturing to the tops of his thighs.

"Why?"

Colin shook his head at her obvious mistrust, but he was smiling. "So I can give you a foot massage."

She hesitated. A foot rub sounded innocent enough, but she knew from experience how dangerous any kind of physical contact with Colin could be.

"Your feet will thank you in the morning," he promised.

Her feet *were* killing her, and his offer seemed genuine.

She turned so that her back was against the arm of the sofa and swung her legs onto the cushions. He slid a little closer, picking up one of her stocking-clad feet in his strong hands. His fingers began to move over the instep, kneading, loosening.

"So how was your…date?" Colin asked, continuing to perform magic on the arch of her foot.

"Fine." She closed her eyes as his fingers worked on her toes. He had great hands. His touch was strong yet gentle, and Nikki was afraid she was going to start moaning in ecstasy. She would never have guessed that a foot rub could be so sensual.

She forced her eyes open, forced herself to think about something—anything—but the way his hands moved over her feet. The way they'd once touched every part of her body.

"You're sure Carly was okay? She didn't give you a hard time?"

"She was great," Colin said, setting down the first foot and picking up the other. "She's a wonderful kid. You've done a good job with her."

"Thank you." Nikki was both surprised and touched by the compliment, and a little wary.

"When I first found out that you'd had a baby—our baby—I was angry. Mostly about how your decision affected me." His hands continued to move over her foot, almost absently, as if the activity somehow made it easier to open up to her. "All I could think about was how much I'd missed out on. I never considered how hard it must have been for you to be on your own."

"It wasn't always easy," she agreed, wondering at his sudden willingness to discuss his feelings.

"Were you scared, when you found out you were going to have our baby?"

"Terrified." She'd never forget how overwhelmed and alone she'd felt. Her marriage had just fallen apart, her mother was still recuperating from a car accident, and then Nikki had learned there was a tiny, helpless life just starting out inside her.

"Did you ever…" He hesitated, and even the movement of his fingers on her foot halted. "Did you ever consider not having her?"

"No." Nikki shook her head, smiled a little. "I'd always wanted to have kids someday. Although I didn't expect 'someday' to come so quickly. Even though you'd decided our marriage was over, I wanted…" Her words trailed off as she realized she was saying too much. Revealing something she didn't want him to know.

He resumed the foot massage. "Tell me, Nicole. I want to know what was in your mind, in your heart."

"I wanted *your* baby," she admitted.

"Why?"

"Because I loved you."

His eyes, tinged with regret and remorse, met hers, and his grip on her foot tightened. "Did you hate me for not being there?"

She didn't want to be any less than completely honest with him now, hoping that maybe he'd understand what she'd been going through when she'd given birth to their child so many years before. "Sometimes. But mostly I was grateful."

He frowned. "Grateful that I wasn't there?"

"No," she said quickly. "Grateful to you, for giving me Carly. She's the best thing that we ever did. She's the best part of both of us."

She smiled wistfully, lost for a moment in her thoughts. "There were so many times over the years that I wanted to call you, things I wanted to share. When Carly cut her first tooth, when she took her first steps, when she went to her first day of junior kindergarten."

"I've missed so much." He sounded wistful.

"You also missed dirty diapers and 3:00 a.m. feedings," she reminded him.

He nodded. "I'm not so sure about the diapers, but I would gladly have shared in the sleepless nights to have had my baby fall asleep in my arms even once."

Nikki's eyes filled with tears. "I *am* sorry."

"What are we going to do now?" He'd finished the massage but still held her feet in his lap, his fingertips skimming lazily up one calf.

"I thought we'd agreed to take things one day at a time."

He nodded.

"Are you getting bored already?"

"I'm not bored," he said patiently.

"Then what is this about?"

"Us."

She shifted to tuck her feet beneath her under the skirt of her dress, trying to put some space between them. The sofa hadn't seemed so small when she'd first sat down. "There is no 'us.'"

"You don't believe that," he chided.

"I do." She lifted her chin.

Colin shook his head and slid across the cushion until his thigh was against her knee. "You have to know that saying something like that is only a challenge for me to prove you wrong."

"No." She put up her hand to ward off his advance.

"If you're convinced that our relationship is over, why do you tremble when I touch you?"

He trailed a fingertip slowly along the swell of her bottom lip, and her involuntary response confirmed his statement. She swatted his hand away. "It's a basic physiological reaction."

His lips curved. "So, according to your explanation, you'd react the same way to anyone touching you?"

Her eyes narrowed, but she said nothing.

"When I kiss you," he continued undeterred, leaning closer to her, "is it the same as any other man kissing you?"

How had they gotten sidetracked on to such things? She needed to direct the conversation back to more neutral territory, but she didn't have any idea how to do that when she was already thinking about the incredible sensations his kisses evoked.

"I don't make comparisons," she said.

"I do," Colin said unapologetically, as he slid one hand up her thigh to cup her hip.

"That's the difference between you and me."

He smiled again, and every bone in her body turned to jelly. Damn him!

"There are plenty of differences between you and me," he drawled. "That's what makes things so interesting. But you missed my point."

"I wasn't sure you had one."

"I did," he assured her. "I was talking about kissing."

His gaze dropped to her lips, lingered there. She felt her breath catch in her throat.

"No other woman I've ever kissed has turned me inside out the way you do. No other woman has haunted me the way you do. So I find it hard to believe you when you say that one kiss is the same as another."

"I don't care what you believe," Nikki said. She was trying for cool disdain, but her words came out sounding strangely breathless.

"Well, I thought we might try a little test."

She didn't need to ask what kind of test he had in mind. She could read the intent in his eyes. He wasn't even trying to mask the hunger that glinted in those green depths, and she knew he could probably see the answering yearning in her own eyes. But she'd learned a long time ago that desires could be curbed, impulses controlled. All she needed was a little willpower.

He leaned a fraction of an inch closer, and the scent of him clogged her senses.

Okay, so what she needed was a *lot* of willpower.

"No," she said firmly.

He smiled. "No what?"

No what? She had no idea. Her mind had gone completely blank and she couldn't think of anything but how much she wanted him to kiss her.

He shifted closer, reached his other arm across her to the arm of the sofa, effectively boxing her in.

"I saw you on the porch," he admitted. "Saying goodnight to my brother."

"You were spying on me?"

"I saw him kiss you." He dipped his head toward her. "Has he ever kissed you—" his mouth brushed against hers, briefly, fleetingly "—like this?"

Then his lips were on hers, moving softly, slowly, seductively.

Nikki felt her eyes drift shut even as her mind instinctively responded. No, Shaun had never kissed her like this. No one else had ever kissed her like this. No one else had ever made her feel the things Colin made her feel.

She felt his arms come around her, draw her closer. This wasn't supposed to be happening, she thought, even as she opened her mouth to the searching thrust of his tongue. But she was helpless to pull away from him, helpless to do anything but kiss him back.

As if of their own volition, her arms wound around his neck. She felt her heart pounding in her chest, matching the rhythm of his. It was as if they were connected—all heartache and deception forgotten. There was no past, no history, no regrets. Only here and now, and a desire that spiraled higher and higher, threatening to escalate out of control.

When he finally ended the kiss, she clung to him, unable to do anything else. She felt empty now, aching with need.

"Look at me, Nicole." Colin's voice was soft but insistent, and she reluctantly raised her eyes. She wasn't sure how it had happened, but somehow she'd ended up in his lap, his arms strong around her. And it felt so right to be there. "Now tell me that you felt the same way when you kissed my brother as you felt just now in my arms."

"I can't," she admitted.

"I fought it for a long time," he said. "This connection between us. I didn't want to admit it was there, that it was anything special. But it is, and it's endured for the more than five years we've been apart. Don't you think that should tell us something?''

His words were even more seductive than his kisses, because he was telling her what she wanted to hear. She'd always believed there was a connection between them—a reason she'd fallen so completely in love with him. A reason she'd continued to love him long after he'd broken her heart.

But that was a lifetime ago—Carly's lifetime, to be precise. She wasn't going to fall for his smooth-talking lines this time. She wasn't going to open up her heart and risk that devastation again.

''It tells me that we shouldn't be kissing.''

''I like kissing you,'' Colin said. ''And I think you like kissing me.''

''That's not the point.''

''It should be,'' he said. ''What's the point of doing something if you don't enjoy it?''

''Colin, please.'' She climbed out of his lap, took a few steps away. She needed space—to settle, to breathe, to think. ''Let's not make this any more complicated than it has to be.''

''You're Carly's mother, I'm her father. It seems pretty simple to me.''

She turned back to him, crossed her arms over her breasts. ''I want us to get along, for Carly's sake. But I don't want anything more than that.''

''I don't believe you don't want me,'' Colin said, rising from the sofa. ''When I kissed you—''

''There was a time when I loved you more than anything,'' Nikki told him. ''I was devastated when you walked out. I won't set myself up for the same heartache again.''

''It would be different this time—''

"No." Her voice was firm, decisive. "It's late, Colin. I think you should go."

But he made no move toward the door.

"I want a second chance for us, Nicole."

Chapter 9

Nikki turned away from him. "I'm not going to be your crutch again, Colin. I can't."

He frowned. "What are you talking about?"

"We met when your career ended. You were at loose ends, not knowing what you would do with the rest of your life. I filled a void for you—for a while. As soon as you got the chance to get back in the arena, you bailed on me and the future you'd claimed you wanted."

"Is that what you think?"

She met his gaze evenly. "That's what happened."

"It's not like that this time."

"Isn't it?"

"No," he denied vehemently. "In fact, I've applied for a job at the new cable station in town."

She moved toward the table and picked up his glass of wine. His kiss had already proved that he was far more dangerous to her system than any amount of alcohol. "You're kidding."

He shook his head. "I go for my screen test Monday."

"What are you going to do with Carly?"

"I'll take her with me."

His quick response surprised her. He was used to doing what he wanted, when he wanted. She'd assumed, obviously incorrectly, that he'd forgotten or overlooked his responsibilities with respect to their daughter.

"What kind of job?"

"Sports commentator."

"Do you really want to give up coaching?"

"I really want to be with you and Carly," he told her.

It was an honest response, if not quite the one she was hoping for.

"How much time is it going to take to prove that I'm here to stay?"

"More than a week."

Colin's lips thinned. "How long?"

"I don't know."

His eyes narrowed. "I made a mistake, Nic. Are you going to make me pay for it for the rest of my life?"

"I'm not trying to punish you."

"It sure as hell feels that way."

"I'm just protecting myself. And my daughter."

"*Our* daughter."

She flushed. "Our daughter."

"I'm not going to walk out on Carly." He took the glass of wine from her and set it back on the table, then linked his hands with hers. "And I'm not going to walk out on you."

"Don't make me any promises," she said wearily.

"I want Carly to have a family."

"I've already said that I won't interfere with your relationship with her."

Colin shook his head. "That's not good enough. I want a chance for all of us to be a family."

She just couldn't do it. She couldn't wipe the slate clean and start over. Even if she wanted to, she wasn't sure it would be possible. And she knew for certain it wouldn't be smart.

She'd welcomed Colin into Carly's life because she hadn't had any other choice—he was her father. But there was no reason she had to let him into her own, and there were a million reasons why she shouldn't. Not the least of which was the vulnerability of her heart.

"Don't you think our daughter deserves the chance to be part of a real family?"

Of course she did, and he knew that she would do anything for Carly. But she couldn't give him what he was asking for.

"All I want is for you to spend some time with me— just the two of us—and time with me and Carly—as a family."

"I don't know if I can."

"I'm not asking for a commitment, just a chance."

"We had our chance five years ago."

"And you're still holding that failure against me."

"No." She sighed wearily. "After I had some time to think about it, I wasn't surprised that our marriage hadn't worked. We didn't know each other well enough to make that kind of commitment."

Colin frowned. "What are you talking about?"

"We got married after dating three months."

"We knew each other almost a year before that."

"We *met* a year before that," she clarified. "But we didn't exchange ten words unless it was to talk about your therapy."

When she'd first met Colin, it had been easy to think of him as just another hotshot jock. Although she knew his injury had ended his playing career, she also knew he'd made more money in that last season than she could hope to make in a lifetime, so it was difficult to feel a lot of sympathy.

She'd turned him down the first time he'd asked her

out—and at least a dozen times after that. His persistence eventually wore down her resistance, though, and when she went out with him that first night, she knew she'd misjudged him. When he'd talked to her about hockey, she'd realized it wasn't just a game to him—or a job. It was his life.

She couldn't help but admire and respect that kind of passion. It might have been luck that he was born with talent, but he'd been smart enough to know what to do with that talent, and courageous enough to pursue his dream.

And that very first night, she'd started to fall in love. She'd given him her heart, freely and completely, believing the love they shared would last forever. She'd been wrong.

"Do you think things would have turned out differently if I'd stayed in Fairweather?" he asked.

She shook her head. "I never wanted you to stay. I wanted you to take me with you."

Colin paused a moment, surprised. "Are you saying that you would have gone to Texas with me?"

"I would have gone to the ends of the earth with you."

"Then give us another chance, Nic."

"We couldn't make it work before," she reminded him. "What makes you think it would be any different now?"

"Because I know now that I'll never feel about anyone else the way I feel about you."

She shook her head again, unwilling to be swayed by his words.

"Do you really expect me to believe that it's over between us? God, Nikki. Every time I kiss you…I don't even know how to describe what I feel. It's never been like that for me, not with anyone else."

"Maybe you haven't let it," she said softly. Just as she hadn't let it. She'd been holding on to the memories of Colin so tightly that she'd never allowed herself to open up to another man. It was the only explanation she could think of for five years of self-imposed celibacy. She refused to believe that she'd never been intimate with anyone else because she'd never stopped loving her ex-husband.

He scowled. "Do you think I haven't tried to forget you? Do you think I haven't wished that I could just get on with my life? Well, I have.

"For years I've been telling myself that whatever we had was over, but I was wrong. You're not a part of my past, Nic. You're a part of *me*. And my life isn't complete without you."

And with those words, her weakened resolve completely collapsed.

"Come on," he said, somehow sensing his advantage. "It's a beautiful night, the sky's full of stars. Why don't we take a walk?"

It was a beautiful night. A night made for romance. A night that could only encourage her to throw logic out the window and follow the perilous yearnings of her heart. She needed to hold on to the logic, tightly, with both hands.

"It's after midnight," she pointed out. "I'm not wandering the streets at this time of night."

"Let's sit on the porch, then." His voice was low, almost irresistible.

"It's been a long day, Colin. I just want to go to bed."

"That's jumping ahead a few steps, but that's okay with me, too," he teased.

Nikki shook her head, but she was helpless to prevent the smile that curved her lips. "Alone."

"Now that doesn't sound like nearly as much fun."

"I need some time, Colin. I need to think, and I can't do that when you're around." When he was near, all she wanted was to say yes—to whatever he wanted. Wherever. Whenever. Preferably hot and naked.

He sighed. "If I let you go, will you be thinking about me?"

"Probably," she admitted, not sounding the least bit happy about it.

"Let me give you something else to think about."

He laid his palm on the doorjamb beside her shoulder and leaned toward her. His body was mere inches from hers, close enough that she could feel the heat radiating from him.

"I'm going to kiss you good-night, Nicole."

Those were the same words he'd whispered at the end of their first date, so many years ago. He hadn't asked. He hadn't given her a chance to refuse. Not that she would have, anyway. She'd been intrigued, infatuated, halfway in love by the end of that first night, and she'd wanted him to kiss her. She'd wanted to feel his lips on hers, his hands on her body.

Of course, she'd had no idea that one kiss would be the start of the most intense and exciting love she'd ever experienced in her life, or that the most brutal and heart-wrenching devastation would follow. Now she knew how fragile her heart was, how dangerous her passion for Colin was, and she had even more reason not to get involved. She had to think about her daughter. She had to be smart. She had to be responsible.

She moistened her lips with the tip of her tongue, saw his eyes darken as they zeroed in on the subconscious motion. Before she could blink, before she could be smart and responsible, he'd breached the few inches that separated his mouth from hers.

Nikki's breath caught in her throat and her whole body seemed to melt. She was grateful for the solidity of the door behind her back, without the support of which she was sure she'd melt at his feet. It wasn't fair that he could make her respond this way with just a simple kiss.

And it was a simple kiss. He wasn't touching her at all except with his lips, but, oh, how he was touching her with his lips. They moved over hers, strong and firm, gentle yet insistent.

Oh God. Three more seconds of this and she'd be pulling him up the stairs to her bedroom, mindless of Carly and Arden and everyone and everything else.

She had to stop this insanity.

Now.

But it was Colin who pulled away.

"I'll see you tomorrow," he said.

As promised, Colin was there the next morning. And the morning after that. Day after day, until Nikki actually started to wonder if he wasn't going to stick around this time.

She was pleased that Colin and Carly seemed to be bonding so well. The obvious closeness between father and daughter helped alleviate some of her lingering guilt. But as her conscience began to clear, she began to worry. She wanted Carly to have a good relationship with Colin, but she couldn't help feeling that the deepening affection between them threatened the mother-daughter bond she'd always cherished.

Even when Nikki had time alone with Carly, which seemed increasingly rare now, Carly was always talking about Uncle Colin. If Nikki suggested going to the park or out for ice cream or anywhere else, Carly always wanted to know if Uncle Colin could come with them. Her daughter's enthusiasm was natural, or so Nikki tried to convince herself, but, there was a part of her that resented the connection between them, that wondered if Carly preferred to be with Colin.

She knew it was an irrational reaction to the situation,

but she couldn't help feeling that Colin was taking her place. He'd become the primary caregiver—the center of Carly's world. And Nikki was afraid if Carly was ever forced to choose, she would choose her father over her mother.

But in the evenings, when Nikki was alone with Colin, just sitting and talking together, her fears would dissipate. At least for a while. And she would allow herself to dream that things could work, that they could be a real family. At the end of each evening, he'd say good-night with long, lingering kisses that made her remember how incredible it had been to make love with this man, and made her want to open her heart up to him again.

On Thursday afternoon of Colin's second week with Carly, Nikki came home from work to find that his rental car wasn't in the driveway. Instead, there was a brand-new, gleaming black Jeep Grand Cherokee in its place.

She got out of her own car and couldn't resist peeking through the window at the spotless leather interior.

"Whose vehicle is that?" she asked, when she found Colin in the kitchen. She heard the theme song for *Cosmic Cat* emanating from the television in the living room, and she knew her daughter wouldn't move from the sofa in the next twenty minutes.

"Mine," he replied.

"What was wrong with the Porsche?"

"That was just a rental." He grinned. "This is *mine*."

She fought against the joy that sparked in her heart. Just because he'd bought a truck didn't mean he was going to stick around for the long haul. A vehicle had wheels; it was infinitely transportable. Colin could use it wherever he went, and to get wherever he was going.

But there was also the large-screen television that had been delivered the previous day. The deluxe climber and swing-set that had taken three men several hours to set up in the backyard Monday afternoon. He'd even bought shoes for Nikki—a pair of high-heeled, silver-colored sandals, just like the ones Carly had ruined.

She'd been absurdly touched by that gift, even more so when Carly had detailed how they'd gone from store to store with her one undamaged shoe looking for a matching pair. But the shoes and the climber and the television were just things, she reminded herself. Colin had always been generous with gifts, free with his money—he could afford to be.

"Do you want to go for a drive?" he asked. "We could go parking up at Lookout Point."

Her lips curved. "The kids up there would think we'd gotten lost."

"Not after we steamed up the windows good."

Why was it that he could tempt her with such a ridiculous invitation? "Why are you doing this, Colin?"

"Doing what?"

"Pretending that you plan on staying, when we both know you can't wait to get out of this town."

"That may have been true at one time," he said, slipping his arms around her waist and drawing her closer. "But things have changed."

"What's changed?" she asked, helpless to keep the bitterness from her voice. "Other than that you don't have a job to run off to."

"A lot of things have changed," he said. "Including the fact that I now have a daughter here."

"Is that going to be enough for you?"

"Probably not," he admitted, his voice low. "Carly is only part of the reason that I want to stay."

She put a hand on his chest as he moved toward her. "Don't, Colin."

"Don't what? Don't tell you how I feel?" He turned away abruptly, raked his fingers through his hair. "Dammit, Nicole. How long are you going to make me pay for being an idiot five years ago?"

"This isn't some kind of retaliation," she retorted. "It's my life."

"All I'm asking is to be part of your life."

"You're in it, whether I want you to be or not."

"Come on, Nic. Can you honestly tell me that you haven't enjoyed the time we've spent together over the past couple of weeks?"

She sighed, because she couldn't. Not honestly, anyway.

His eyes narrowed. "I'm not going to walk out on you this time. Sooner or later, you're going to have to acknowledge that truth."

"Time will tell." She turned to walk away, but he caught her wrist, held it. The familiar zing of awareness skated up her arm, arrowed straight for her heart.

He put his other hand on her waist and turned her around so that she was facing him. "You don't have to be afraid, Nicole."

She stiffened, but her eyes were steady on his. "I'm not afraid. Just cautious."

He pulled her closer, skimmed his hands up her spine. "Does being cautious keep you warm at night?"

He grazed her earlobe with his lips.

"Does it make your body tremble with anticipation?"

He touched his tongue to the pulse point at the base of her jaw.

"Does it make you scream out in pleasure?"

She put a hand on his chest, but she didn't push him away. "Don't," she said again.

"Don't what? Don't remind you how good it was between us?"

"Don't make me want something I can't have."

"We could have it all, Nic."

She shook her head. "It's too soon."

"And I was thinking that it's taken us far too long to get to this point." He smiled ruefully and brushed a strand of hair from her cheek. "But I didn't mean to pressure you."

She gave him a wry smile. "Yes, you did."

"Maybe just a little," he admitted.

"I really want to believe this would work," she told him.

"Then let yourself," Colin murmured. "Believe in me. Believe in us."

Then he kissed her, and Nikki closed her eyes and let herself at least consider the possibilities. Not the least of which was taking Colin upstairs and spending some quality time with him in her bedroom.

But that would be extremely dangerous. Because she knew she couldn't give him her body without opening her heart. And she'd vowed to protect her heart at all costs.

She didn't see any harm in a few little kisses, though. Even if his kisses did make her bones melt and her heart pound against her ribs so hard she thought they might crack.

"You guys should get a room," Arden's voice interrupted.

Nikki pulled away from Colin, her face flushed like a schoolgirl's. Well, better Arden than Carly, she thought. She was still answering questions about that kiss in the kitchen their daughter had interrupted.

"Actually," Colin said, not the least embarrassed about the lip lock they'd been in when Arden entered the room. "I was just trying to talk Nikki into taking a drive in my new Jeep."

"It looked more like your tongue talking to her tonsils," Arden said dryly.

He grinned. "Her tonsils were resisting the idea."

Nikki cleared her throat. "Could you two please stop talking about me as if I wasn't in the room?"

"Just go for the ride. All this sexual tension in the air

is unhealthy for the rest of us,'' Arden said, causing Nikki's cheeks to heat again.

It was time, she decided firmly, to assert control over the situation. ''Carly,'' Nikki called to her daughter. ''Do you want to go for a ride in Uncle Colin's Jeep?''

Colin's cocky grin slipped a notch. ''I am not taking you up to Lookout Point with a four-and-a-half-year-old in the back seat,'' he muttered under his breath.

Nikki's smile was just a little smug. ''Exactly.''

The Cone Zone was a busy place on a Thursday night. Of course, the unexpected heat wave that had blanketed the town with ninety-degree temperatures for the past few days probably hadn't hurt the business any.

Boomer parked beside a snazzy black Jeep and reluctantly left the climate-controlled interior of his borrowed vehicle to join the line of patrons that extended through the open door of the restaurant. His shirt was sticking to his back before he'd even crossed the parking lot, and he took a handkerchief from the pocket of his shorts to wipe the perspiration from his brow.

The line slowly inched forward until he was finally inside, out of the blinding sun and oppressive heat. He perused the menu behind the counter as he wiped his brow again. There were too many flavors, too many choices. He liked things to be simple. Unfortunately, nothing had been simple since he'd signed on for this thankless assignment.

He turned his attention from the item list to the customers milling around. Mostly teenagers, he noted, in pairs or larger groups, and a few families. The couple in front of him had their arms wrapped around each other, their hands in one another's back pockets. He couldn't imagine wanting to get that close to another human being in this stifling heat.

Shaking his head, he focused his attention on the party

directly in front of the groping adolescents. A man and a woman with a child—a little girl—standing between them.

His assessed the male figure critically. Approximately six feet tall, muscular build, medium brown hair. Were the eyes shaded behind those dark sunglasses green? It was impossible to tell, but the rest of the description was close enough to hold his attention.

The teenagers moved away with their sundaes and the trio stepped up to the counter.

"One double scoop of Pralines 'n' Cream, one double Chocolate Cookie Crunch, and..." The man looked down at the little girl. "What are you going to have, Carly?"

"Strawberry!"

"And a single strawberry."

"Double, Uncle Colin."

Colin. The sound of the name released a quick jolt of adrenaline through his system.

"Okay," the man called "Uncle Colin" relented, then he grinned at the child before turning back to the server. "Make that a double scoop of strawberry."

"Please," the child reminded him.

"Uncle Colin" smiled. "Please."

Boomer smiled, too.

The target had finally been confirmed.

Chapter 10

Colin parked across the street from the police station, then sat in his vehicle for a long moment, the scrap of paper weighing heavily in his pocket. He was probably overreacting. He was almost certain of it. But as often as he tried convince himself of that fact, he couldn't shake the feeling that he was being followed.

It was like a strange tingling at the back of his neck. An uncomfortable sensation that stole over him at times, an eerie suspicion that he wasn't alone. Paranoia, most likely, brought on by Parnell's threats and the deaths of three innocent people. The first time he'd experienced the feeling, he'd noticed a dark blue Honda behind him on the way to his brother's house. He hadn't thought too much about it at the time, but he was sure he'd seen the same vehicle at least three times since then. Most recently Friday morning when he'd taken Carly to the park.

While he might be willing to disregard his intuition and take chances with his own life, he wouldn't risk anything happening to his daughter. So he'd called the precinct to find out when Detective Creighton would be working.

Colin had played minor hockey with Dylan Creighton when they were kids, and they'd remained friends—if not close—through high school. Of course, Colin had left Fairweather soon after to play professional hockey and Dylan had enrolled in the police academy.

He'd seen Dylan infrequently on his trips home over the years, which meant not at all in the past five years. But Colin knew it would be easier to share his concerns with an old friend than a complete stranger.

"Colin McIver." Dylan rose from his desk and extended a hand. "I'd heard a rumor you were back in town."

Colin accepted the proffered hand. "For a while, anyway."

"I haven't seen you since the judge's funeral."

"I haven't been back since then," Colin admitted.

The detective sat back down behind the scarred metal desk. "This is your first trip home in more than five years?"

Colin just shrugged. "I've been busy."

"I've been following your team," Dylan told him. "You had a great season."

"Until the play-offs," Colin agreed.

"There's always next year."

But Colin wasn't sure there would be a next year. Even if the new owners wanted to renew his contract, Colin wasn't sure he wanted to go back—not if it meant leaving his daughter behind. Three weeks earlier, he hadn't even known he had a child. Now he couldn't imagine his life without her.

"Although I'd like to think you just dropped by to say hello, it looks like you've got something on your mind," Dylan said.

"Yeah. It's probably nothing but…"

"What's probably nothing?"

Colin took the scrap of paper out of his pocket and passed it across the desk.

"License-plate number?"

He nodded. "Of a dark blue, late model Civic hatchback."

Dylan scribbled the details and license-plate number on a scratch pad.

"It's probably just a coincidence," Colin said, "but I've noticed the vehicle on a few occasions. Almost as if the driver is following me." And although he believed it was a coincidence, he couldn't take the chance. He couldn't risk anything happening to Nikki or Carly.

"Do you have any reason to suspect that someone would be following you?"

Briefly Colin explained about Duncan Parnell's threats, the bomb in his condo, the incident at the hotel in Baltimore, Parnell's escape from custody, and the more recent and unsettling feeling that he was being followed, along with specific sightings of the vehicle.

"All of this because you benched the kid in the playoffs?"

Colin just nodded. It was easier than explaining the whole story—the car accident over the Christmas break that had wrecked Parnell's back, his intensive therapy, the nonprescription medication he'd relied on to help him play through the pain. Colin hadn't realized how bad Parnell was still hurting until Gil Beauchamp—a teammate of Parnell's and one of his closest friends—had told him, and Beauchamp had only confided in Colin because he was concerned that Parnell was popping more and more of the little white tablets to make it through a game.

It was almost the end of the season when he'd confronted Parnell about the drugs. Parnell had tried to dismiss the concerns, claiming that he just needed a little something to take the edge off the pain. Colin blamed himself for not having seen the symptoms sooner, and he knew the only way to help Parnell—to force the kid into treatment for his addiction—was to scratch him from the roster. He'd regretted the decision ever since.

Dylan shook his head. "And they say being a cop is dangerous."

Colin just shrugged.

"Can you tell me anything else about this vehicle?" Dylan asked.

He thought for a moment. "I don't think so."

"What about the driver? Male or female?"

"He hasn't been close enough for me to get a good look, but I'm pretty sure he's male."

"I'm sure you're right," Dylan agreed. "If it was a female, you'd have her phone number instead of her license-plate number."

"And I wouldn't be giving it to you," Colin retorted.

The detective grinned. "I'll check this out for you."

He left the police station reassured that Dylan would take care of the situation, allowing Colin to concentrate on reuniting his family.

The key in convincing Nikki that he would be there for her and Carly, Colin decided, was to back up his words with action. She'd had more than five years for the resentment and distrust to grow; he couldn't expect to overcome those negative feelings overnight. It would take time and perseverance to change Nikki's mind about who he was and what he wanted. It was a good thing he had plenty of both.

He knocked on the back door at the preappointed time for their trip to the zoo Saturday morning, anxious to get started on his campaign. A family outing—hopefully the first of many—would be a great opportunity to show Nikki that he wanted to be a family.

But when Nikki opened the door, she didn't appear to

be ready to go to the zoo or anywhere else. His eyes flickered over her. The leggings and oversize T-shirt she wore looked as if she'd slept in them, and the tousled hair and bleary eyes suggested that she'd still been sleeping when he'd knocked.

Even disheveled, she managed to look sexy, reminding him of just how she'd looked when she'd crawled out of their bed after a night of passionate lovemaking. He cleared his throat. "You're not ready."

"I'm sorry." She smothered a yawn with the back of her hand as she stepped away from the door to allow him entry. "I meant to call you first thing, but…" Her words trailed off, her brows drew together. "I don't even remember hearing the alarm."

"You look like you've had a rough night," Colin said, noting the dark shadows under her eyes, the fatigue in her shoulders.

"I did," she agreed. "We all did. Carly was sick last night, and Arden and I took turns sitting with her."

He experienced a quick flash of panic. "Is she okay?"

Nikki nodded. "I'm sure she will be."

"Was it something I did?"

Her brow furrowed. "What?"

"I was with her all day yesterday. I must have fed her something—or done something—or maybe I forgot to do something—"

"Colin." Nikki spoke to him sharply, then softened the harsh interruption with a weary smile. "You didn't do anything wrong. Kids get sick every now and again, and Carly just happened to choose last night to do it."

"Are you sure?" He wanted to believe her, but he couldn't help thinking that his lack of fathering skill was somehow responsible for the onset of his daughter's illness.

"I'm positive. There's some kind of virus going around, and Carly picked it up."

"I took her to the park. She must have got it from one of the other kids there."

"It wasn't your fault," Nikki assured him.

He wasn't convinced. "How is she now?"

"Sleeping," she said, and stifled another yawn.

"You should be, too," he told her.

She shook her head. "I just need coffee."

"You need to rest."

"I need to be with Carly, in case she wakes up and wants something."

"I'll stay with her," Colin offered. It was the least he could do.

"Carly's not in any shape for a visit right now," she told him.

"You're not in any shape to fight with me," he pointed out.

"Why are you doing this?"

"So that you can get some rest. The last thing you need is to pick up Carly's bug because you've allowed yourself to get run down."

"I've been taking care of myself for several years now," she told him.

"I'm sure you have," he agreed. "But I'm here, and I'd like to help out." It wasn't quite how he'd planned to spend the day, but it was an opportunity to prove to Nikki that she could count on him.

"Why?"

He sighed. The woman was too stubborn and independent for her own good. She couldn't just accept help when it was offered; she had to make everything into a battle of wills. Well, this was one battle he had no intention of losing. "Go to bed, Nikki."

She scowled at him.

"I'll sit with Carly. We'll watch TV, eat some chicken soup."

He could tell she was tempted but still reluctant to give in.

"Please," he said, "let me do this. Go have a nap. When you wake up feeling better, you can boot me out."

That, at least, earned a small smile.

"If you need anything—"

"I'll manage," he interrupted.

Still she hesitated. "Are you sure? She's been throwing up on and off for the past ten hours."

Okay, so this revelation took the edge off his enthusiasm, but he was determined to do this. To prove himself as a father, to prove himself to Nikki. "Does she have a bucket?"

Nikki nodded.

"Then we'll be okay."

She continued to look skeptical, but she nodded. Of course, she went into the living room first, checked Carly's temperature, and pressed a kiss to their daughter's flushed cheek before heading up the stairs to her own bedroom.

Nikki hadn't planned to sleep more than an hour—all she needed was a quick nap to rejuvenate her system. But she was almost asleep before her head hit the pillow, and the next time she opened her eyes it was two o'clock— nearly four hours since Colin had shown up and shooed her off to bed.

She knew she should check on Carly, but she figured if there were any problems Colin would have woken her. So she took a quick shower, put on clean shorts and a cotton sweater, and was feeling a lot better by the time she ventured back downstairs.

She tiptoed through the living room, where Carly was asleep on the sofa, and into the kitchen where the scent of fresh coffee greeted her. There was no sign of Colin anywhere. Nikki pulled a mug out of the cupboard.

Surely he wouldn't have gone back to his apartment and left Carly alone, even if she was sleeping.

She poured herself a cup of coffee, then followed the sound of running water to the laundry room. What she found there made her wonder if she wasn't still dreaming, and what a fantasy it was!

Broad shoulders, firm pectorals, rippling abs. Olive-colored shorts sitting low on narrow hips, over long, muscled legs lightly dusted with dark hair. Above the flawless body, a face that women would sigh over and men would envy.

And he was doing her laundry.

Ironing, in fact. Even she didn't usually bother pressing her blouses but hung them up as soon as they came out of the dryer. The image of Colin, so strong and blatantly masculine, with an iron in his hand, was something she'd never forget.

"He makes great coffee *and* he irons," she said.

Colin's head jerked up, then he smiled. "How are you feeling?"

"Much better, thanks." She gestured to the ironing board. "That's not necessary."

He lifted his broad shoulders in a shrug, and it was all she could do not to drool as the muscles across his chest flexed in response to the action. "I was just waiting for the dryer to finish."

"Is your shirt in there?"

"Yeah. Carly had a little accident."

"Just one?" Nikki asked, hoping to hear that their daughter was over the worst of whatever ailed her.

But Colin shook his head. "Only one missed the bucket."

"How long has she been asleep?"

"Almost two hours." He slipped her blouse onto a hanger, expertly fastening the top button with one hand.

Nikki lifted her mug to her lips, sipped. He did make

great coffee, and it was safer to concentrate on his skill in the kitchen than to let herself remember how he'd *un*buttoned her clothes with the same practiced ease. ''Can I get you a cup of coffee?'' she offered.

''I'll get it,'' he said, and bent over to unplug the iron. The motion caused his shorts to stretch enticingly across his buttocks.

Nikki quickly retreated to the kitchen. She seated herself at the table and watched Colin move around the room as if it was his own. He found a mug for himself and filled it from the carafe.

''Are you hungry?'' he asked.

''Starving,'' Nikki admitted.

''Do you want me to make you an omelette or something?''

''It's my house,'' Nikki reminded him. ''I think I can find something to eat. And I think I'm feeling well enough to kick you out now.''

''You're going to kick me out without feeding me?''

Nikki sighed. ''I guess I do owe you some lunch.''

''You don't owe me anything,'' Colin said. ''But I wouldn't mind a sandwich, if you're so inclined.''

Nikki found some cold meat and cheese in the refrigerator and busied herself making sandwiches. She would feed him, thank him again and send him on his way. There was no reason to feel all hot and disconcerted just because Colin was looking at her as though she were on the menu.

She cut the sandwiches, set two on a plate for Colin, one on another for herself.

He picked up a piece of sandwich, grinned. ''Quarters?''

''Habit,'' she explained. ''That's how Carly likes hers.''

''I'll have to remember that,'' he said, then took his first bite.

Nikki nibbled on her own sandwich, finding her appetite for lunch stifled by a stronger appetite for the man seated across from her.

The buzzer on the dryer sounded just as Colin was finishing his sandwich. When he returned from the laundry room a few minutes later, he had his shirt on again. Nikki felt a pang of disappointment that his fabulous chest was covered, but he still looked too sexy for his own good. Too sexy for her peace of mind.

She pushed away from the table to gather up their plates.

"Do you mind if I hang around a while longer?" he asked.

Nikki hated herself for weakening at the obvious plea in his voice. "Are you telling me you don't have anything better to do?"

"I was planning to spend the day with you and Carly," he reminded her.

"I'm sorry your plans were ruined," she said.

"They weren't ruined, just amended."

Nikki laughed softly. "Now that's an understatement if I've ever heard one."

He smiled. "Isn't this part and parcel of what it means to be a parent? The good, the bad, and the vomit?"

"Yeah," she agreed, then smiled.

"Mommy?" The call was thin, weak.

Nikki dropped the plates into the sink and hurried into the living room, where Carly was lying on a mound of pillows on the sofa.

"How are you feeling, baby?" She touched the back of her hand to Carly's forehead, relieved to find that the fever seemed to be subsiding.

"I'm thirsty," Carly said.

Colin, having anticipated her complaint, came into the room carrying a plastic cup of ginger ale with a flexible straw. "Here you go, Squirt." He handed the pop to Carly.

She took the cup and drank thirstily.

Then promptly threw up all over herself and the blankets wrapped around her before she could reach for the bucket. And she started to cry.

Nikki stripped off Carly's pajama top, then pulled her onto her lap for a cuddle. Colin scooped up the soiled blankets and clothing and took them to the laundry room while Nikki carried their daughter upstairs for a quick bath.

When Carly was dry and dressed in clean pajamas again, Nikki took her back downstairs. Colin was picking up the crayons and papers that were scattered on the coffee table. She smiled when she heard the faint whir of the washing machine in the background.

Both Nikki and Colin sat with Carly to watch one of her favorite videos, then they fed her some chicken soup and a few soda crackers. By the time Carly fell asleep again, both her parents were almost ready to drift off, too.

"Hopefully she'll have a better night tonight than last," Colin said, after Carly had been tucked into her own bed.

"Hopefully," Nikki agreed.

"I should take off, so you can get some rest, too."

She nodded, although she was no longer as anxious to get rid of him as she had been earlier. She wouldn't have asked for his help, but she'd appreciated it. It had been nice to share her worries and concerns with the father of her child. "Thank you…for being here today," she said. "And tonight."

"I'm glad I could be," he said. "I imagine you've been through far too many days like this on your own."

"A few," she admitted.

"I wish…" His voice trailed off and he shook his

head. "It doesn't matter. I'll give you a call tomorrow to see how Carly's doing."

Nikki nodded. "Okay."

She walked with him to the door, wondering what he'd wanted to say, and why he'd changed his mind. Had he wished he'd been there for his daughter? Would things have been different if he'd known about Carly?

She gave herself a mental shake. He was right. It didn't matter. The past was just that, and wishes couldn't change anything.

Colin traced beneath her eye with a fingertip. "You have shadows here." He brushed a strand of hair off her cheek, tucked it behind her ear. "Your hair's standing up." His fingers trailed down her arm, then laced with hers. "And you are still the most beautiful woman I've ever known."

Oh God, how was she supposed to keep her heart intact when he kept battering away at her armor like that?

She pulled her hand from his, turned to unlock the door. Even as she knew their relationship had been inevitably moving toward intimacy again, she needed to maintain some level of control. She wasn't ready to give him everything. Not this time. Not yet.

And that was why she needed to get him out of her house.

Now.

Because her emotions—concern for Carly, gratitude for Colin's help and support, lust for his body—were threatening to drown out the rational part of her brain that was supposed to keep reminding her why a relationship with Colin was a bad idea.

When she turned around again, Colin was right in front of her, her back against the door.

"I have to kiss you," he said.

She put her hand on his chest. "You have to go home."

"Not until I kiss you."

It took all of her willpower to keep her eyes open and focused. She couldn't let him kiss her. If he did, she knew she'd be lost. "Now," she said, hating the unsteadiness of her voice.

"Right now," he agreed.

That wasn't what she meant, and he knew it. But his lips were already on hers, and she was unable to protest any further. His mouth moved over hers, firm yet gentle. Intoxicatingly familiar. She heard a soft moan and knew it had come from somewhere deep inside of her. As much as her head knew she needed to keep her distance from Colin, her body and her heart had entirely different ideas.

She needed to pull away from him. She'd promised herself that she wouldn't do this. Then his hands slipped under her sweater and up her back, and she melted against him. No one else had ever made her feel like he did. No one made her want or need like he did. She knew he'd be leaving again; she couldn't allow herself to hope that he might stay this time.

But he was here now.

Would it be so wrong to take what he could give her while he was around? They were both consenting adults, and so long as she kept her eyes open, so long as she didn't delude herself into thinking that they had a future together, there was no harm in letting this attraction between them follow its natural course.

So decided, when he eased his lips from hers, speaking the next word seemed more natural to her than breathing.

"Stay."

Chapter 11

Colin's breath strangled in his throat.

Had Nikki just asked him to stay?

As if responding to his unspoken question, she tilted her head to look up at him. "Stay," she repeated, her soft gray eyes unwavering.

Okay, maybe he was an idiot, but he wanted to be sure what she was asking. He wanted to make sure that *she* knew what she was asking. "Why?"

Her teeth sank into the fullness of her bottom lip. "I didn't think I'd have to spell it out for you."

"You want to have sex with me?"

"Yes."

Her quick, unhesitating response should have pleased him. Instead, it left him feeling oddly disappointed. "No."

"No?" She looked stunned, then hurt.

Colin shook his head. "I'm not going to have sex with you." He slid his hands over her ribs until they rested just below the curve of her breasts. "But I will make love with you."

She raised her eyebrows, as if to suggest that the distinction was irrelevant. But they both knew it wasn't. She'd been holding back from him for the past couple of weeks, and he wouldn't let her hold back any longer. He wanted her to open up to him completely: body, heart and soul. He wanted to make love to her slowly, endlessly, until she could no longer deny that they were meant to be together.

"Forget it," she said. "It's late anyway, and Carly will be up early in the morning."

Her response didn't surprise him. She was running scared—unwilling to admit the strength and invincibility of what was between them. "What are you afraid of, Nicole?"

"I'm not afraid. I just don't want to make a big deal out of something that isn't."

He ignored the quick stab of pain her words evoked. He understood that she was lashing out in an effort to protect herself. "Making love *is* a big deal," he said, his voice low and husky with promise. "And making love with you is an incredible pleasure."

Her brows drew together in a frown. He lifted one of the hands that spanned her waist and gently rubbed his thumb over the scowl until the lines smoothed out. Her eyes, when they met his, were dark with emotion. Desire. Temptation. Need. And underneath it all, wariness.

"I want to keep this simple, Colin."

"Then we'll keep it simple," he promised, before his mouth covered hers again.

It was a kiss filled with passion and promise, and she softened, yielded, in response. His lips skimmed down the column of her throat, and her head fell back in surrender, her sigh no more than a whisper. He stroked his tongue over her skin, savoring the taste of subtle seduction that was uniquely Nikki. His hands moved slowly over her now, drawing out her response rather than demanding it. And respond she did, with dreamy kisses, soft murmurs and gentle caresses.

"Are you sure this is what you want?" It nearly killed him to pull back enough to even ask the question, but he needed to be sure. He didn't want her to have any regrets after the fact. "I don't want to rush you, Nicole."

Her breathing was labored, her eyes smoldering as they met his. "If I was any more ready, I'd explode."

He grinned against her lips. "I'm counting on it."

He started to lift her sweater.

"Bedroom," she panted. "Upstairs."

"Upstairs," he agreed, and lifted her off her feet as he headed toward the staircase. She wrapped her arms around his neck, her legs around his waist, and held on as he carried her up the stairs, continuing to tease her with his lips, his tongue, his teeth.

"First door on the left," she told him, gasping the information between kisses.

He pushed open the door with his foot, then shouldered it closed behind them, still tantalizing her with his kisses. He flipped on the light switch, illuminating the two lamps that flanked either side of the Queen-size sleigh bed. Later he might appreciate how thoroughly seductive the setting was. Now, his only concern was getting Nikki naked and on top of that bed.

He unwrapped her legs from around his waist, and as she slid down the front of his body, the soft curves of her body rubbed the hard angles of his own. He was helpless to suppress the groan that rumbled deep in his throat.

"We don't need the lights," she said, reaching toward the nearest lamp.

He caught her hand, turned it over and pressed his lips to her palm. "Yes, we do," he said. "I want to see you."

He finished unfastening the tiny buttons on the front of her sweater, and slipped it from her shoulders. Beneath it, there was nothing but Nikki. He cupped her breasts in his palms, heard her soft gasp of pleasure. He stroked his thumbs over her nipples, felt them pebble in response to his caress.

Clothing fell away quickly, and they came together again, flesh to flesh, seeking, demanding, responding.

He lowered her onto the bed, knelt over her, continuing to cherish her with his hands and his lips. He touched her with infinite care and tenderness, arousing her slowly, completely. He reached out to her, with his body, his lips, his heart. He wanted to tell her that he loved her, but he knew she wasn't ready to hear the words. She wouldn't believe them. So he showed her instead. With every kiss and caress, he showed her how much he loved her, needed her.

He felt her body shudder beneath him as the first orgasm ripped through her. He swallowed her cries of pleasure, continuing to touch her, driving her toward the peak again.

"Colin, please."

The words were a whispered plea, and he was more than happy to comply with her request. Since that day in his hotel room, he'd accepted and welcomed the inevitability of this moment, and he'd made damn sure he'd be prepared for it.

He covered himself quickly with a condom then rose over her, and in one deep thrust, buried himself inside her. He felt her muscles contract around him, watched her eyes glaze, as he began to move. Slowly at first, long, deep strokes that reached through her body to her very soul.

Her hips rose to meet his, again and again, in a perfectly choreographed mating dance. Here, at least, there were no barriers. No lies, no history. Nothing but the two of them, joined together, moving as one.

The tempo increased, faster, faster, driving them both to unimaginable heights of pleasure. She locked her legs around his waist, pulling him deeper, deeper, into the slick heat of her core, until he could hear nothing else over the roar of blood in his head. He held tightly to the little bit of control he had left until he felt the spasms begin to wrack her body. Then he tumbled over the edge with her.

Nikki lay silently beside Colin, her heart still pounding against her ribs, her skin still flushed with pleasure. She wasn't sure how long they remained tangled together on top of the sheets. Minutes? Hours? It didn't matter. She was too drained to move. Too satisfied to want Colin anywhere but exactly where he was, on top of her. The feeling of rightness was so strong, so all-encompassing, it almost managed to check the sense of panic growing inside her.

Almost.

With a soft groan, Colin lifted himself slightly to roll off her and landed face down on the mattress. He turned his head to nuzzle her throat, draped an arm across her waist. "I thought I remembered how good it was between us," he murmured. "I was wrong."

She had been, too. The memories that had haunted her didn't begin to compare to the reality of making love with Colin.

She didn't regret being intimate with Colin again. It was hard to have regrets when her body was still trembling with the aftereffects of pleasure. But she was worried. She'd wanted to hold back, to keep her heart intact. Instead she'd given him everything: her body, her heart, her soul.

Not that he'd given her much choice. He'd been so

tender and patient, his hands and lips almost reverent as they'd explored every inch of her body. Holding back had not been an option. Bit by bit, she'd felt her control slip away, her heart melt.

She loved making love with Colin.

She loved Colin.

Nikki stiffened, the dreamy recollection jolted by an icy dose of reality. Of course she wasn't in love with Colin. Thinking she was in love just because they'd shared incredible sex was a predictable but inaccurate reaction to the situation.

As if sensing her tension, Colin stroked a hand lazily down her spine. She exhaled slowly, forced herself to relax.

"Having second thoughts already?" he asked.

"No. I was just…um…thinking that I should get a drink…of water."

"Okay." But he tightened his arm around her, brushed his lips over hers.

She closed her eyes and melted into the kiss.

"Water," she said, belatedly remembering what she'd planned to do. "I'm going to get some water."

"Okay," he said again, lifting his arm so she could climb off the bed.

She found her robe in the closet, wrapped it around herself and slipped out of the room.

She didn't really need a drink. What she needed was some distance to think about the situation. But she filled the cup and put it to her lips.

Everything would be okay, she assured herself, so long as she didn't start thinking about happily ever after. She and Colin were both consenting adults engaging in a mutually satisfying affair. She would enjoy it for as long as it lasted, and move on with her life when it had run its course. There was nothing wrong with sharing a physical relationship with Colin so long as she kept her heart out of it.

Nikki sighed and refilled the cup, forced to admit, at least to herself, that it was too late to protect her heart. Whether she wanted to be or not, she was already emotionally involved with Colin. He was her ex-husband, the father of her daughter, the only man she'd ever loved. The only man she'd ever love.

Oh, hell. She'd gone and done it again. She *had* fallen in love with Colin.

Where were her self-preservation instincts when she needed them? How had she allowed this to happen?

She sighed, recalling the awestruck wonder on his face when he first saw Carly, the complete contentment as he watched her perform some menial task, his infinite gentleness when he held her. How could she not love the man who so evidently loved their daughter?

As if that wasn't enough to make Nikki tumble head over heels, there was the way he looked at her, as if she was the only woman in the world. The way he touched her, as no one else ever had.

"You look deep in thought."

Nikki turned to her cousin. "I didn't hear you come in."

"Obviously," Arden said. "Is everything okay? Is Carly all right?"

"She's fine. Or better, anyway."

"Then why are you looking so pensive?" her cousin asked.

"Nothing, I—"

"Actually," Arden interrupted, "you don't look pensive so much as...dreamy."

Nikki flushed. "You're being ridiculous."

Arden lifted a brow. "Am I?"

"Yes, I'm just thinking about Carly."

"Really?" Arden smiled as she heard footsteps coming down the stairs. Straining to peek through the doorway, her smile broadened. "If I had someone like that warming my bed, you can bet I wouldn't be thinking about anything else."

Nikki felt her cheeks burning. "It's not…" She started to say that it wasn't what Arden was thinking, but the truth was, it was probably *exactly* what Arden was thinking.

"Never mind," she muttered as Colin came into the kitchen, wearing only a pair of shorts riding low on his hips.

"I just wondered what was taking you so…" His words trailed off as he spotted Arden. "Oh, hello, Arden."

She nodded her acknowledgment. "Colin."

"Arden was just going to bed," Nikki said pointedly.

"All right." But she turned to Colin. "Remember, if you mess this up again, I'll have to track you down and hurt you."

"Arden," Nikki said again.

Her cousin shrugged unapologetically and sauntered out of the room.

Nikki set her glass back on the counter, turned to Colin. "I'm sorry," she apologized. "Arden likes to pretend she's my big sister."

Colin slipped his arms around her waist, drew her toward him. "She's just looking out for you, as I'm sure you would do for her."

"Yes, but…"

"But?"

"I don't want you to think that I have any… expectations. As far as our…relationship, is concerned."

"Why wouldn't you have expectations?"

"I just meant…" She exhaled audibly, searching for

the words to explain what she meant. Gave up. "This is awkward."

"It doesn't have to be," he told her, then closed his mouth over hers.

She responded to his kiss. There were some aspects of their relationship that weren't awkward at all.

"We should talk about this," she said when he'd ended the kiss.

"Later," he promised, and swept her into his arms to carry her back upstairs.

Colin had never realized how much he wanted a family until he'd started spending time with Nikki and Carly. *His* family. It didn't matter that he and Nikki were divorced, or that Carly didn't know he was her father. The only thing that mattered was that they belonged together, and he believed they deserved a second chance to be a family. Lying beside Nikki in her bed, he was even more convinced of that fact.

The biggest obstacle—disregarding for a moment the threats against his life—would be convincing Nikki. It seemed that no matter what he did or how hard he tried, she was still waiting with bated breath for him to announce that he was leaving again.

He'd never been the type of person to take things one step at a time. It had always been his philosophy to go after what he wanted, no holds barred. That was how he'd pursued Nikki the first time.

But she wasn't the same woman anymore, he wasn't the same man he'd been five years earlier, and the stakes were much higher this time around. He didn't just want Nikki; he wanted their daughter. He wanted them both to be his. Forever.

He knew Nikki had put up barriers around her heart. Self-preservation was a natural instinct. But the attraction between a man and a woman was natural, too, and whatever difficulties and mistrusts they had yet to overcome, there was no denying the strength of the chemistry between them.

As he lay beside Nikki in the darkness of her room, their bodies still slick and heated from lovemaking, he knew that he didn't want just her body—he wanted her heart. Completely and unconditionally.

"Are you going to let me stay tonight?" He was still on top of the covers, Nikki cradled close to his side. He skimmed his fingers over the slope of her hip, down her thigh. She had an amazing body—firm and supple and incredibly responsive.

Nikki shook her head. "I don't want Carly to wake up and find you here."

He could understand her concerns, but he didn't want to go. He didn't want to let her go. Because he knew that the minute he was out the door, she'd start to think, and she'd think of a hundred reasons why their making love had been a mistake.

"How about if I set the alarm to get up at four o'clock?" he suggested, nuzzling her throat.

"Carly might wake up in the night."

"Does she usually?"

"No," she admitted. "But if she did…"

Colin sighed. "Okay, Nic. I'll go."

"Thank you." She pressed her lips to his, then sighed into his mouth when he deepened the kiss. She wriggled against him, aligning her hips with his, and Colin's body responded immediately.

"Didn't you say something about wanting me to go?"

She wrapped her legs around him, drawing him back to her. "Later."

It was much later before he thought about leaving again. Nikki had fallen asleep in his arms, but he stayed beside her, content to just hold her in his arms.

Why had he ever given up this indescribable sense of

peace and completion for a job that had taken him half-way across the country from the woman he'd loved? If they had the next fifty years together, he knew he would always regret those five years they'd been apart. Just as he knew he had no one but himself to blame for the loss.

He also knew that he would dedicate every day of the rest of his life to proving to Nikki how much he loved her, if only she would give him a second chance. Despite his current position in her bed, he knew that nothing had changed between them. She was still wary and distrustful, and he was still an out-of-work former hockey player who didn't have a lot to offer—except that he loved her.

When he found his eyes growing heavy, Colin reluctantly eased himself from the bed and found his discarded clothing on the floor. He dressed quietly, then pulled the covers up over Nikki. She stirred but didn't waken.

He dropped a kiss on her forehead and whispered into the darkness of night the words he knew she wasn't ready to hear.

"I love you, Nicole."

Then he slipped out into the night, too preoccupied with thoughts of Nikki to notice the dark blue sedan parked across the street, the curl of smoke drifting through the partially open window or the shadow of the man watching.

Chapter 12

It was a struggle for Nikki to make the transition from sleep to wakefulness after getting precious little rest the night before. She remembered dozing off in Colin's arms at one point after they'd made love, and then waking with a start, instinctively knowing that he'd gone. Although it was what she'd wanted, she found it difficult to fall back to sleep again without his warmth beside her. Instead she'd lain awake for a long time, thinking about their relationship.

They never had gotten around to discussing their expectations, or lack thereof, and that worried her. Maybe she should have thought about setting the groundwork before she'd fallen into bed with him last night, but she'd been so relieved that Carly was feeling better, and so grateful to Colin for being there to help her through it, and—

Oh, hell. Who was she kidding? She'd just wanted to jump his bones.

But today was another day, and she knew it was important to reestablish some boundaries. Making love didn't make them a couple, and she had no intention of centering her life around him again. She was determined to enjoy what they had, for so long as they had it, and she wanted Colin to understand that she didn't harbor any expectations of a future together.

She pushed off the covers and found her robe on the floor at the end of the bed, where Colin had tossed it after he'd slipped it from her body. Before he'd made love to her again. Just the memories caused her blood to heat, her skin to tingle, and she again felt a twinge of regret that she hadn't let him stay. It might have been nice to wake with him beside her, to make love with him as the sun was coming up.

She wrapped the robe around herself, knotted the belt at the waist, then went in to check on Carly before heading downstairs for a much-needed cup of coffee. She pushed open Carly's bedroom door, found the bedding in a tangled heap, the bed empty, and her daughter's pajamas in a pile on the floor.

Pleased that Carly was feeling well enough to be up and about already, Nikki followed the scents of fresh coffee and frying bacon as she made her way down the stairs.

It was rare for Arden to cook. She was a good lawyer but a culinary disaster. Every once in a while, though, she'd attempt breakfast. Usually pancakes or French toast, and usually at Carly's request.

Nikki sniffed. It didn't smell like anything was burning. Yet.

But when she stopped at the doorway to the kitchen, she saw that Arden wasn't cooking breakfast today. She was seated at the table with a mug of coffee between her hands, and Colin was standing over the griddle.

Something in Nikki's chest expanded, making it difficult to breathe. He looked so natural in her kitchen, with

Carly sitting on the countertop a safe distance from where he was cooking but close enough that she could supervise the chef's activities.

Nikki closed her eyes. It was all too easy to imagine that this scene was a normal occurrence, that Colin was going to stay around and be a permanent part of their lives. But because she knew he wasn't, because she knew this couldn't last, she locked the memory into her heart with all the others she'd been collecting over the past couple of weeks.

"Can you make Kitty Kakes?" Carly asked, as Colin poured more batter onto the pan.

"Kitty Kakes?" he echoed dubiously.

"It's like a cat-shaped pancake," she explained. "It gives Cosmic Cat her super powers."

"Oh." He scowled at the pan.

Nikki tightened the belt of her robe and stepped into the kitchen. A man who couldn't draw a dog on paper couldn't be expected to make a cat with pancake batter. "I'll do it," she said, crossing to the grill.

Colin turned to her, smiled as his eyes skimmed over her. The warmth of his gaze was as tangible as a caress, and equally unnerving. "Good morning," he said huskily.

"Morning," she repeated, shooting a quick glance at her cousin, who seemed enthralled by the contents of her coffee cup.

She kissed Carly's forehead and noted that it was cool to the touch. "Morning, sweetie. You must be feeling better."

"I'm *starving*," Carly told her.

Nikki smiled. Carly had managed to eat very little the day before; she'd managed to keep even less of it in her stomach.

"We were going to bring you breakfast in bed," Carly

said, sounding only a little disappointed. "But I'm glad you're up, 'cause now I get Kitty Kakes."

Colin flipped the pancakes that were already on the grill. Then stepped back and handed the plastic pitcher of batter to Nikki.

"What are you doing here?" she asked.

"I told you I'd come by in the morning to see how Carly was feeling," he reminded her.

"I didn't think you meant at the crack of dawn." Nikki poured a small amount of batter on the grill to form a head, a larger amount for the body, then added two drops for ears and a thin tail.

"It's after nine o'clock," he chided. "Hardly the crack of dawn."

"I've never known you to be an early riser."

His breath was warm on her earlobe as he leaned closer and whispered, "That's because I never had an incentive to get out of bed so long as you were in it with me."

She stepped away from the grill, certain it was the heat from the stove that had caused her skin to flush. "Whose idea was it to make pancakes?"

"Mine," Carly piped up.

"But it was my idea to bring you breakfast in bed," Colin said, his voice pitched low enough that only she could hear. "I was hoping to find out if you still sleep in the nude."

"Not with my daughter in the house," she assured him, then turned to the daughter in question. "How come you're dressed already?"

"Auntie Arden's going to take me to her office to play on the 'puter, then we're going to a movie."

Nikki selected a slice of bacon. "I don't think you should be going anywhere. You were very sick yesterday."

"But I'm all better today," Carly assured her.

Nikki glanced at her cousin.

"I thought it might be good for her to get out of the house, and for you to have some time to yourself. Very low-key activities." Arden grinned. "For us, I mean."

Nikki turned back to the griddle, nibbling on the bacon as she flipped Carly's pancake. She and Colin had to talk about what happened last night. His appearance here this morning, and Arden and Carly's unquestioning acceptance of it, concerned her. Not that she wasn't happy to see him, but she didn't want to start expecting him to be there. She didn't want to count on him.

She dished up Carly's pancake and set the plate in front of her daughter. Carly picked up the syrup with both hands and drowned her pancake in it.

Nikki shook her head but said nothing. She nipped another slice of bacon from the plate and poured herself a mug of coffee.

"Aren't you going to eat?" Colin asked her as he prepared his own stack of pancakes, smothering butter between each layer and flooding syrup over the top.

It amazed her to realize how much Carly was like her father, particularly in ways that she would have assumed were learned behavior. Like the aversion to cauliflower, and the fondness for maple syrup. Apparently the McIver genes were stronger than she'd given them credit for.

"Nic?" Colin said.

"What?"

He shook his head and leaned across the table to pile three pancakes on her empty plate. He started to tip the bottle of syrup, but Nikki snatched it from his hand.

"I'll do it."

He knew his way around a kitchen, Nikki decided after the first bite. It was something she hadn't known about him when they were married. Or maybe he hadn't learned to cook until later.

She cut another wedge of pancake. It would be easy enough to get used to this special treatment, to imagine finding him in her kitchen every morning, and in her bed every night. She swallowed, but the pancake seemed to lodge in her throat. She picked up her mug and gulped down a mouthful of coffee.

No, she was not going to start envisioning a long-term future with Colin. She couldn't risk her heart and her dreams again.

"I'm all done, Mommy." Carly wiped the syrup off her face with a paper napkin.

Nikki glanced at her daughter's empty plate. Carly was obviously feeling better today. "Did you have some juice?"

Carly nodded. "Apple. Can me an' Auntie Arden go now?"

"After you brush your teeth."

"'Kay." She hopped down off her chair. "Do you want to come with us, Uncle Colin?"

Nikki had opened her mouth to decline her daughter's invitation before she realized it hadn't been issued to her. She snapped her jaw shut, vaguely registered the sound of Colin's voice as he responded to the question.

It was ridiculous to feel hurt, she chided herself. It wasn't as if she *wanted* to go out with Arden and Carly, but that wasn't the point. The point was that Carly had always included her, but this time she'd chosen to invite Colin instead.

Nikki drained the last of her coffee then pushed away from the table and carried her dishes to the sink. She was being childish and irrational, and she knew it. But she'd been the center of Carly's world for so long, and she hadn't been prepared for that to change. Not yet. She felt as though her role had been usurped by Colin, that she'd been replaced in their daughter's affections. And Carly didn't even know that he was her father.

When they told Carly the truth, would she choose to be with Colin instead of Nikki? And what if Colin decided to leave Fairweather? What if he had a chance to coach again? Would he want to take Carly with him?

She didn't think he'd be able to, not without her consent. But what if Carly wanted to go?

"Nic?"

She started. "Sorry. Did you say something?"

"Are you okay?"

She forced a smile. "Fine. Why?"

"You looked kind of…panicked."

That wasn't surprising, considering that she was feeling kind of panicked. But she wasn't prepared to share her fears and insecurities with Colin. She wasn't sure she could trust him not to take advantage of the situation.

"I'm a little worried about Carly," she said instead. "I really think it would be better if she stayed home today."

"Whatever she had was probably just a twenty-four-hour bug that's run its course."

She frowned. When had he become such an expert?

"You can make her stay home," Colin said. "But she won't appreciate it."

Nikki sighed, knowing it was true. "Did you set this up?"

Colin shook his head as he nudged her aside to pour dish soap into the basin and turn on the water. "Not that I'm complaining about being left alone with you, but no, I can't take the credit for it." He left the faucet running and reached for the knot of her belt. He tugged on it, pulled her closer. "But I had decided that I wasn't going to give you too much time or space to think about last night."

Nikki wished he'd at least give her enough space to breathe. She couldn't think when he was crowding her, and judging from the gleam of satisfaction in those dreamy green eyes, he knew it. Damn him. Her blood started to hum, her pulse to race, and her concerns about their daughter were pushed to the back of her mind.

"Are you wearing anything under this excuse for a robe?"

She swallowed. "Of course, I am."

He slipped open the knot, parted the fabric and found the thin silk chemise. "You wear something like that to sleep alone?"

"It's comfortable," she said, all too aware that she sounded defensive.

He pulled the robe together as the sound of footsteps descended the stairs. She grasped the belt and knotted it.

"We'll be gone most of the day," Arden said as she helped Carly tie her shoelaces.

Nikki shook her head. No one could ever accuse Arden of being subtle. But she knew her cousin's intentions were good. She gave Carly a quick hug and a kiss. "Don't eat too much popcorn."

"Don't nag." Arden said, ushering Carly out the door.

"Now that you have the morning free, what do you plan to do?" Colin asked, brushing his lips down the column of her throat.

Nikki shivered and stepped away from him. She feigned a yawn. "I think maybe I'll go back to bed."

"Is that an invitation?" Colin stepped forward, bridging the distance she'd put between them. He opened her robe again, skimmed his hands from her waist to the hem of her chemise.

"No," she told him. He slid his hands under the silky fabric, up her thighs. Her breath hitched. "Maybe."

Colin grinned and lowered his head to cover her lips, while his hands continued to move upward, doing all kinds of wonderful things to her body.

"Yes?" he prompted, brushing his thumbs over the peaks of her tightened nipples.

"Yes," she agreed breathlessly.

* * *

Wednesday afternoon, Colin met Dylan Creighton for coffee at a little café downtown.

"You didn't tell me you were staying with your ex-wife," Dylan said, when Colin slid into the booth across from him.

Colin also hadn't told Dylan to keep his visit between them, and he mentally cursed himself now for the oversight. If Nikki had even an inkling of his suspicions, she would be furious with him. And rightly so.

"Did you go to the house?"

The quick shake of Dylan's head alleviated his immediate concerns. "I drove by," he said, "but opted not to stop in when I saw Nikki outside."

"I appreciate your discretion."

Dylan nodded. "She had a little girl with her. Yours?"

Colin couldn't help but smile. "Yeah."

"Cute kid."

His smile widened. "Yeah," he said again.

"Looks just like her mom."

Colin chuckled at the good-natured gibe. "Lucky for her, she does."

"I take it Nikki doesn't know you came to see me?"

"I thought I'd wait to see what you turned up on the owner of the car before I sent her into a panic." And before she sent him packing, which she would undoubtedly do if she suspected he'd been followed to Fairweather. Not that Colin could blame her. She'd expressed concerns right from the beginning, and he'd discarded them.

Now he'd know if that had been a mistake. "What did you find?"

Dylan grinned. "A terrified eighteen-year-old kid who thought I was going to haul him off to jail."

"I take it you didn't."

"Nah."

"He wasn't following me?" Now Colin really felt like an idiot.

"He was following you," Dylan said, "trying to work up the nerve to approach you for an autograph."

"You're kidding?" The sense of relief was almost overwhelming.

His former teammate grinned. "Not at all. In fact, he's waiting outside in his car, hoping to meet you."

Colin chuckled again. "Tell him to come in."

Dylan walked out of the coffee shop, returning a few minutes later with a tall, skinny kid whose face was almost as red as his hair.

"Colin, this is Eddy Luchyshyn. Eddy, meet Colin McIver."

"It's a pleasure to meet you, Eddy."

Colin wouldn't have thought it was possible, but the kid's face flushed even deeper. "M-Mr. McIver."

"Eddy saw you play against the Flyers nearly a dozen years ago," Dylan explained on behalf of the tongue-tied teenager.

"Did we win?" Colin asked.

"Five-two," Eddy said solemnly. "You scored two goals."

"You've got a great memory."

The kid beamed proudly. "It was the first game my dad ever took me to."

And it had obviously meant a lot to Eddy. As it would have meant a lot to Colin to have shared such father-son moments with his own dad. But Richard McIver had always been too busy to make time for his sons, too important to care. Colin pushed the resentment aside.

"Do you go to a lot of games?" he asked.

"We used to go to a few every year. But it's the first one I remember most clearly."

Colin knew what he meant. He understood the importance of firsts: the first time he'd put on his Tornadoes jersey, his first NHL goal, his first play-off game. And Nikki—his first love. The one woman he'd never forgotten; the woman he still loved.

He forced his attention back to the young man in front of him. "Are you still a Flyers' fan?"

The spark in Eddy's eyes dimmed a little. "I didn't really follow the team this year…after my dad got sick."

"He's in the hospital," Dylan explained, obviously having checked out and confirmed the kid's story.

"I…um…I have the program from that game," Eddy said.

Colin smiled as he took the crumpled booklet from the kid's outstretched hand. It had been a long time since he'd been asked for an autograph, longer still since anyone had looked at him with the kind of admiration he saw in Eddy's eyes. When he'd lost his career, he thought he'd lost everything. He'd loved living in the spotlight, but only now did he realize that he didn't even miss it anymore.

"Would you—would you sign it for me…for my dad, please?" Eddy asked.

"I can do even better than that," Colin told him.

He wasn't sure what compelled him to make the offer, but as he exited the Fairweather General Hospital a short while later, Colin was glad he'd done so.

Robert Luchyshyn had been as thrilled as his son to meet Colin, his enthusiasm barely dampened by the disease that ravaged his body. Bone cancer, Eddy had told him before they entered the room. The doctors expected that he only had a few weeks left to live.

Despite this prognosis, the man had been in good spirits as his wife sat on one side of his bed, his son on the other. And Colin couldn't help but envy Robert Luchyshyn the close bond that he shared with his family. He was a man who'd loved and been loved, and he would be missed deeply when he was gone.

That was the true legacy, Colin suddenly realized. What mattered weren't career accomplishments or social status or money and possessions, but the touching of other peoples' lives and the memories that would remain.

It was something his father had never learned. Or maybe Richard McIver hadn't cared. He'd made his mark in the judicial community—the respect and attention of his colleagues more important to him than any relationship with his own sons.

There had been a time, not so long ago, that Colin might have been guilty of the same narrow-minded focus. But not anymore.

He'd come to Fairweather to escape the danger stalking him, thinking of nothing beyond that immediate concern. It was only when he'd seen Nikki again that he'd started to question the choices he'd made. Then he'd come face-to-face with Carly, and in that first moment of recognition, everything had changed for him.

His visit to the hospital only served to remind him of the importance of living every moment to the fullest. And he was determined to do just that.

Nikki was in the backyard pulling weeds out of the flower bed when he got home. She was kneeling in the dirt, her denim cutoffs stretched enticingly across her softly rounded bottom, her sleeveless top clinging to the gentle curve of her breasts.

He crossed the yard in a few quick strides and pulled her to her feet.

"Colin, what—"

It was as far as she got before he covered her mouth with his own in a brief but potent kiss.

"What…" She brushed her hair away from her face with the back of her hand, leaving a smudge of dirt on her cheek. "What was that for?"

He rubbed his thumb over the trace of mud. "Because I love you."

Her eyes widened for a second before she schooled her features into a carefully neutral expression. "Have you been drinking?"

"I've never been more sober," he assured her.

She continued to eye him warily.

Colin didn't blame her for her reservations, he just wished he could find some way to get past them.

It had been almost a week since they'd resumed the physical aspect of their relationship, and he'd spent every night since in her bed. Correction: he'd spent *part* of every night in her bed, but Nikki always insisted that he sleep in his own apartment.

If he'd believed that her concerns about Carly finding him in her bed were genuine, he wouldn't have minded so much. But he couldn't shake the feeling that Nikki was using their daughter as a convenient excuse to avoid the intimacy of actually sleeping with him.

She was more than willing to make love with him. She held nothing back physically, but her emotions remained carefully guarded. Not only was she not willing to open up her heart, she visibly withdrew whenever he tried to tell her how he felt about her. Like now.

But this time he wasn't going to back down. This time, he was going to make her understand the choices he'd made, the regrets that haunted him, and the feelings that were still in his heart.

He led her over to the pair of Adirondack chairs so they could sit down. He had a feeling this could take a while.

"Do you remember when we met?" he asked.

If Nikki was surprised by his abrupt change of topic, she didn't show it. She nodded.

"You were the first therapist assigned to help me with my rehab after a shattered kneecap ended my career—

the one bright light in my otherwise dismal existence. And from the first time we met, I knew you would make the difference in my life.''

''Obviously we have very different memories of that meeting.''

He grinned at her dry tone. ''What do you remember?''

''A sullen, temperamental jock who made it clear he wasn't the least bit interested in therapy.''

''I wasn't. What was the point when the doctors said I'd never play professional hockey again? ''I didn't want the therapy,'' he admitted. ''But I wanted you.''

She sent him a look of patent disbelief.

''I did. I even found myself looking forward to the physio sessions, just to see you. I'd never had trouble meeting women while I was playing hockey, but when I lost my career, I lost my identity and my self-confidence.''

''You found your confidence again soon enough.''

One corner of his mouth turned up in a half smile. ''It's a good thing, too,'' he said. ''Because you kept turning me down when I asked you out.''

''We had a professional relationship,'' she reminded him. ''Personal involvement was inappropriate.''

''Then why did you finally say yes?''

''I felt sorry for you.''

Her answer stunned him. ''You felt sorry for me?''

She shrugged. ''I figured you must have been pretty desperate to keep asking.''

''Maybe I was just persistent.''

''Maybe.''

''Did you marry me because you felt sorry for me, too?''

''No,'' she admitted after a short hesitation. ''I married you because I loved you.''

It was what he'd wanted her to remember, but he hadn't expected the memory to make her sad.

He cradled her face in his palms and looked deep into her eyes. "I still love you, Nicole. And one of these days I'm going to convince you of that fact."

Chapter 13

Two days later, Colin's words continued to echo in her mind. *I still love you, Nicole. And one of these days I'm going to convince you of that fact.*

It wasn't just the words, it was the sincerity in his eyes, the determination in his voice that both thrilled and terrified her.

She wanted to believe that he loved her. She wanted to believe it was possible that he loved her even half as much as she loved him. That was the problem. Because this was exactly how she'd felt when she'd fallen for him the first time.

Okay, maybe not *exactly*. This time, everything seemed more intense, more real. And that just made it worse. Because this time not only could he break her heart, he could break Carly's, too.

Nikki was puzzled as she turned the knob of the back door and found it locked. Then she remembered that Colin had made plans to take Carly to Philadelphia for the day, to visit the children's museum and take in a baseball game. Nikki didn't mind that they'd gone, and she knew Carly was in good hands with her daddy, even if their daughter didn't yet know that Colin was her father.

Nikki's original concern about keeping that bit of information from Carly had long since waned. Colin had more than proved his willingness to share in all the joys and responsibilities of parenthood. He *was* Carly's father, and he deserved to have that relationship acknowledged.

She slipped her key into the lock and stepped inside. The house was unnaturally quiet without Colin and Carly waiting for her, without the television blaring in the living room. Not peaceful, really, just empty.

She had moved to the refrigerator to consider her options for dinner when she heard a car in the driveway. She peeked out the kitchen window, knowing that Colin and Carly wouldn't be home for hours yet, and still hoping that Colin's Jeep might pull into view.

Instead, it was his brother's Lexus. She fought the surge of disappointment. She hadn't had a chance to visit with Shaun since the night of the clinic fund-raiser, and his company might be just what she needed now to get her mind off her ex-husband.

"Business or pleasure?" she asked, when she met him at the door.

"Both." He kissed her cheek, then handed her a large manila envelope.

"That was quick," Nikki said. "Thanks."

He waved off her thanks. "I aim to please. Although I don't think this is necessary."

"What do you mean?"

"Come on, Nic. You and Colin have been inseparable for the past couple of weeks. Why don't you just marry the guy and put him out of his misery?"

"He hasn't asked me to marry him," she replied

matter-of-factly, although just the thought stirred flutters of cautious hope in her heart.

"Then my brother doesn't have half the brains I give him credit for." Shaun grinned. "Marry me, and let's watch him wallow in misery for the rest of his life."

Nikki laughed. "It's a tempting offer, but I think I'll pass."

"Yeah." He shrugged. "I kind of thought you might."

"I wouldn't turn down your company, though, if you wanted to stay for dinner."

"Are you on your own?"

"I am. Colin took Carly to a baseball game tonight, and Arden is at a late settlement conference."

"In that case," Shaun said, "I would love to stay for dinner."

When Colin arrived home with Carly after the ball game, Nikki was waiting on the front porch. But she wasn't alone. Shaun was with her, and they were sitting side by side on the porch swing. Nikki's head was against the back of the seat, almost, but not quite, resting on his shoulder.

Colin assured himself that there was no reason for the slow burning in his gut. He and Nikki were very definitely involved, and despite her continued insistence that there were no strings to their relationship, he knew she wouldn't encourage his brother's attention while she was sleeping with him.

He pulled his Jeep alongside Nikki's car in the double driveway. Carly, exhausted from the excitement of the baseball game, had fallen asleep in the back seat before they were halfway home. He chose to ignore his brother's unexpected presence for the moment and focused his attention on getting Carly out of the vehicle without disturbing her slumber.

He opened the back door and the interior light illuminated her sleeping form. Her head was tipped forward, her hair curtaining her face. He leaned across her and unbuckled the seat belt, tipping her head back gently. Her eyes were closed, her lashes fanning her cheeks, her little rosebud lips slightly parted.

He watched her for a moment, still amazed to think that he'd had any part in creating this amazing child. He eased her from the seat and into his arms. She curled into him easily, trustingly, and his heart went to mush.

Closing the door quietly so as not to startle her, he carried her toward the front porch.

He passed Carly into Nikki's waiting arms. Their daughter stirred and yawned, but her eyelids never flickered.

"I'll get her changed and into bed," Nikki whispered.

As she went inside to settle their daughter, Colin turned to his brother. "What are you doing here with my wife?"

"Your *ex*-wife," Shaun clarified, sounding almost amused.

Colin's eyes narrowed. "Answer the question."

"I stopped by on my way home from work, and Nikki invited me to stay for dinner."

"Why are you still here?"

"We've been talking," his brother explained.

"Just talking?"

Shaun snorted. "What did you think—that we were groping one another in the dark until you pulled up?"

Phrased that way, so crudely and bluntly, the question forced Colin to acknowledge the absurdity of his inquiry. Except that Arden suspected Shaun had feelings for Nikki. And then there was that kiss he'd witnessed.

"I just wanted to make sure you weren't putting any moves on her. Like the night you went to that fund-raiser thing."

He still didn't remember what Nikki had called it, but

he did remember—very clearly and in minute detail—
how she'd looked in that shimmering dress she'd worn.
He remembered the burning jealousy in his gut when his
brother had kissed her.

"Saw that, did you?" Shaun grinned. "I should have
figured you'd be peeking through the curtains."

"You're lucky I didn't toss you off the porch," Colin
muttered. "Of course, I could always do it now."

"You could try."

"Don't tempt me."

"I never thought Nikki was the type to be impressed
by brute strength, but she did marry you once." Shaun
shrugged. "I guess there's no accounting for taste."

"And what kind of woman suits your taste?"

"I'm not particular."

"Well, go find one of your own," Colin said. "Nikki's
mine."

His brother set the swing in motion again. "I didn't
see a ring on her finger."

"Back off, Shaun."

Apparently unfazed by the warning, Shaun stretched
his arms over the back of the chair. "Yeah, a woman like
Nikki might be worth brawling over. I seem to recall that
I could take you more often than not when we were
younger."

"When we were kids," Colin scoffed. "Now you wear
a suit to the office, and the most exercise you get is your
weekly squash game."

Shaun rose to his feet, and looked down the four inches
he had over his younger brother. But Colin stood his
ground. They were pretty evenly matched in weight despite the differences in their height, and he was almost
itching for an excuse to take his frustrations out on his
brother.

It had been too many years since he'd worked off
steam in a good fight. Of course, on the ice it was a five-

minute penalty; on the street, it could be deemed assault. But his brother didn't worry him. Shaun might make his living spouting off about the law, but he wouldn't hide behind it.

"That comment was just condescending enough to make me want to prove a point," Shaun said. "But I don't think Nikki would appreciate having to mop up your blood off her porch. Besides, she's too blind in love with you to know she's making a mistake. Again."

Colin's irritation died almost as quickly as it had risen. "Do you think so?"

"That she's making a mistake?"

Okay, maybe the annoyance hadn't completely dissipated. He glared at his brother. "Do you think she loves me?"

Shaun shook his head. "Man, you're just as love struck as she is. It's almost embarrassing to watch the two of you make gaga eyes at one another."

Gaga eyes? Ordinarily a statement like that would have earned his brother at least one good punch, but hope expanded in Colin's chest, pushing everything else aside.

Shaun laughed. "If I wasn't so happy for you, I'd hate you."

"Have you and Nikki..." He hesitated. "Were you ever...involved?"

"No. I might have considered it at one time," Shaun admitted. "But I don't think she ever got over you."

Colin's relief was palpable.

"That doesn't give you license to screw up again," his brother warned.

"I have no intention of screwing this up," he said solemnly. "I love her, more than I ever thought it was possible to love somebody."

"So why are you telling me instead of her?"

"I've tried telling her. It hasn't seemed to make much difference."

"Give her time. Prove to her that she can trust you."

Colin sighed. He'd thought that's what he was doing. He spent his days with Carly, his nights with Nikki. He'd thought they were growing closer, that she was learning to trust him again.

But when he'd told her he loved her the other day, she'd looked stunned, scared. Not that he'd expected a reciprocal declaration. But he had expected more of a reaction than what she'd given. And her apparent dismissal of his love had struck him deeply.

Never had another woman had the power to hurt him. Or to heal him.

He needed Nikki. He knew now that his life was incomplete without her in it. He'd been a fool to have ever let her go, and he wouldn't make the same mistake again. This time, he planned to hold on to her forever.

Except that he couldn't make any plans for forever until he knew for sure that the threats against his life had passed and his presence wouldn't endanger either Nikki or Carly. The realization frustrated him, and at the same time made him all the more determined to live each day to the fullest.

Colin forced his thoughts back to the present, and the annoying problem of his brother's continued presence. "Don't you have somewhere else to be?"

Shaun grinned. "Nope."

Colin's steely-eyed glare would have sent a lesser man scrambling; Shaun only chuckled. But he did move toward the steps.

"All right, I'm going. Tell Nikki I'll talk to her later."

"Much later," Colin muttered.

Shaun was still laughing as he climbed into his car.

"Where's Shaun?" Nikki asked when she came back outside a few minutes later and found Colin in the swing his brother had occupied earlier.

"I sent him to find his own woman," Colin said.

"To find—what?" Nikki seemed torn between amusement and indignation.

"His own woman," he repeated. He stopped the gentle motion of the swing and tugged on Nikki's wrist to pull her down beside him. "I'm tired of finding him with mine."

"With…yours?" she spoke slowly, carefully.

Colin laid his arm across the back of her shoulders and leaned in, his mouth hovering above hers. "You are my woman."

When her eyes lifted to his, he saw that hers were spitting fire. "Just because I'm choosing to sleep with you at the present time does *not* make me your woman."

Colin clucked his tongue against the roof of his mouth in a sound of disapproval. "If you were being honest, you'd admit that neither one of us gets any sleep when we're together."

"Having sex doesn't make me your woman," she amended testily.

He moved a fraction closer, until he could feel the warmth of her breath mingle with his own. "Making love with you makes you mine." He brushed his lips over hers. "And it makes me yours."

Her arms came around his neck, and she pulled his head down to hers to kiss him more firmly.

"Well, then," she said, when she released him so they could both catch their breath. "As long as we're on equal terms."

"Always," he promised her.

There was nothing Boomer hated more than baby-sitting detail, and that's what this latest assignment had turned into. He'd been following the target around for what seemed like forever, determined not to lose sight of him now that he'd been found.

Under ordinary circumstances, the job would have

been done already and he would have been long gone from this little nowhere town. But it had taken Parnell a few days to come through with the funds, and a few days more for Boomer to track down a supplier.

Even now, his source wasn't certain he could procure the necessary materials. Boomer had given him a twenty-four-hour deadline, after which he'd look elsewhere.

In the meantime, he was keeping an eye on the target. Today, that necessitated a trip to the zoo.

Boomer hated the zoo. He hated the crowds and the noise and the animals and the stench. He tossed the cardboard box toward a nearby trash can. And he hated the stale popcorn.

Most of all, he hated wasting time.

Efficiency wasn't just an asset in his line of work but a necessary rule of survival. Move in quickly, blend into the background, do what needed to be done and get out. He never stayed in one place long enough to become recognizable, and he knew he'd already been here too long.

He paused in front of the enclosure where a Siberian tiger was sleeping in the sun, oblivious to the passersby. He wished he could block out the crowd as easily. He wished he could be anywhere but here.

Soon, he promised himself. Soon it would all be over.

He moved on, an unsettled feeling in the pit of his stomach that it wouldn't be soon enough.

As they wandered through the zoo Sunday afternoon, Carly's endless energy and boundless enthusiasm continued to amaze Colin. They'd been going for hours, and while both he and Nikki were showing definite signs of fatigue, their four-and-a-half-year-old daughter wanted to go back and see the monkeys "just one more time." Which would make it the sixth time already. But they followed without protest as Carly turned in the now familiar direction of the primate compound.

After Carly finally had her fill of the chimpanzees and the gorillas and all species in between, they headed through the throngs of people toward the exit. Colin made a brief stop at the gift shop on their way out and bought Carly a stuffed monkey with a garishly colored face.

She squealed with delight when he handed her the surprise, and Nikki rolled her eyes—as he'd known she would. She was always cautioning him against giving Carly everything she wanted, and more. But he figured he had a lot of years of gift giving to make up for.

To soften Nikki's disapproval, he pulled a second monkey out of the bag and handed it to her. She blushed as she accepted the offering, but he knew she was pleased with the gift when she kissed him in front of the masses of people milling around them.

Okay, it was a brief peck on the cheek, but it had to mean something. Especially since she'd refused to let him hold her hand as they'd strolled around the grounds, concerned that Carly might get "ideas" about the relationship between the two of them. Colin had decided to humor her, even though he figured their daughter was smart enough to know that he was head over heels in love with her mother.

He figured days like today—easy, lazy days that they enjoyed as a family—were just the ticket to easing Nikki toward the realization that she could be in love with him, too.

They stopped at a family restaurant off the highway to grab a bite to eat before going home. The diner was crowded and noisy, and as Colin glanced at the chaos around them, he couldn't help but smile. When he and Nikki had been dating the first time around, they'd shared wine by candlelight. Tonight it was milk under glaring fluorescent light, hamburger instead of filet mignon, and paper napkins rather than linen. And he was enjoying himself immensely.

At least until he turned to speak to Carly and caught a glimpse of the man seated a few tables away. He was sure he didn't know the man, and yet something about him was oddly familiar.

"Colin?" Nikki touched his arm, drawing his attention back to his own table. "Is something wrong?"

"No." He shook salt onto his fries, glanced at the solitary diner again. "Do you know that man?"

"What man?"

"The one sitting by himself in the corner."

She looked in the direction indicated, shrugged. "He doesn't look familiar. Why?"

"I think I saw him at the zoo today."

She laughed. "There were hundreds, if not thousands, of people at the zoo today. How could you remember one man?"

Nikki was right. The zoo had been crowded—with couples and families and tour groups. Which was precisely why this man had stood out. He'd been alone, wandering by himself in the midst of the couples and families and tour groups, yet always seeming to be close to Colin and Nikki and Carly.

Or maybe he was just imagining it, as he'd imagined that Eddy Luchyshyn was stalking him. He shrugged off the sense of unease, certain he was being paranoid again. But he breathed a silent sigh of relief when the solitary diner paid his check and left the restaurant.

Chapter 14

Carly fell asleep in the Jeep again on their way home from the restaurant. She didn't even stir as Colin carried her into the house. He and Nikki worked together silently, getting their daughter changed out of her clothes and into her pajamas. Colin tucked her into bed, Nikki tucked Emma under her arm, and they both kissed her good-night.

"I can't believe the way she just crashes like that." Colin followed Nikki out of the room. "She seems to go, go, go—full steam ahead. Until she runs out of steam."

Nikki nodded and smothered a yawn with the back of her hand. "I think I've about run out of steam, too."

Colin tugged her toward the sofa, lowered himself onto it and pulled her down onto his lap. She didn't resist but laid her head against his shoulder. "You've had a busy weekend."

She nodded again.

He rubbed a hand over her bare thigh. "My new bed was delivered yesterday."

She tipped her head toward him, smiling. "I don't know why you needed a new bed—you spend most of your time in mine."

"Except that you kick me out before dawn every morning."

"You know why."

"Yeah, I know." He didn't agree with her reasoning, but he was acquiescing for now. Time and patience, he promised himself.

He dipped his head to kiss her softly. "Anyway, I thought you might want to take a closer look at the bed."

"That sounds...tempting. But Carly's upstairs and—"

"Arden's back," Colin reminded her. He skimmed his lips over her cheek, nibbled on her earlobe.

"I can't just..."

Her explanation faltered when he nuzzled her neck, the stubble on his chin rasping her sensitive skin.

"Okay," she agreed.

Colin didn't give her a chance to change her mind. He lifted Nikki off the couch and led her through the kitchen, where Arden was standing at the counter making a sandwich.

"Carly's asleep upstairs," Nikki began. "So we were just going to...um...go down to Colin's for...a while," she finished lamely.

Arden finished cutting the sandwich, then turned around and smiled. "I saw the new bed."

Nikki's face flushed scarlet, but Colin just grinned. He figured Arden was smart enough to know he and Nikki didn't spend their nights playing euchre behind her bedroom door.

"We won't be gone long," Nikki said.

Arden lifted an eyebrow and turned to him. "I don't know, Colin, but I think she just insulted you."

Colin wrapped an arm around Nikki's waist and half

dragged her toward the door, anxious to escape before she could disparage him any further.

"Don't wait up," he told Arden.

He heard her laugh as the door closed behind them.

Nikki's eyes widened when Colin opened the bedroom door and stepped aside for her to enter. The new king-size bed dominated the small room, the dark plaid cover turned back to reveal crisp navy sheets. "It's huge."

Colin grinned. "Now why couldn't you have said *that* in front of Arden?"

The corners of her mouth kicked up. "I am sorry about that."

But he was already tugging the T-shirt out of her shorts, unconcerned about her earlier comments. Then his hands were on her skin, and she wasn't thinking about anything but getting him naked and on to that massive bed.

He pushed her shorts over her hips and lifted her against him. She wrapped her arms around his neck, her legs around his waist, and they tumbled together onto the bed just as the phone started to ring.

Colin ignored it, his hands and lips moving over her.

"Shouldn't you…um…get that?" Nikki asked.

"Get what?"

Get what? How was she supposed to remember when he was doing such wonderful things to her body. Then it rang again, a jarring reminder.

"The phone," she said breathlessly.

"I'm kind of busy right now."

"Yes, but…it might be…important."

He raised his mouth from her breast to look at her. His eyes were dark and heavy with desire.

"*You* are important, Nicole." He whispered the words against her lips, his hands moving over her curves with tantalizing slowness.

Her eyes drifted shut as the answering machine clicked on. Colin's voice instructed the caller to leave a message, and then another voice—deep and male and unfamiliar—came through the speaker.

"Colin, it's Ian." There was a pause, and then, "Colin, if you're there, pick up the phone."

Colin reached over her head, and she thought he was going to lift the receiver. But he just turned off the speaker, and the voice disappeared. The intrusion forgotten, he gave her the benefit of his complete and undivided attention.

Nikki had almost gotten used to the heat, the passion. But there was something else now. Something more. It terrified her as much as it thrilled her. His kiss was slow and devastatingly thorough, his lips moving over her cheeks, her jaw, feathering soft kisses on her skin.

He was, she realized with some surprise, seducing her. While she thought it was a sweet gesture, she didn't need a seduction. She only needed him. She reached for him, wanting to feel his body on hers, in hers. But he wrapped his hands around her wrists and drew her arms up over her head while he continued to kiss her. The position brought his body more firmly against her, flattening her breasts beneath the solid wall of his chest, creating a spiraling ache at the juncture of her thighs where she could feel his erection pressing against her.

"Colin...please..." She wasn't sure whether she was asking him to continue or to end the exquisite torture. She hadn't even realized he'd released her hands until she felt his own skimming over her skin. His fingertips brushed the sides of her breasts, and she shuddered—she might even have whimpered. She couldn't be sure. She wasn't sure of anything except that she'd never felt so cherished as she did in his arms at that moment.

His hands continued their painfully slow journey over the curves and contours of her body, relentlessly stoking the fire that simmered inside her. She was ready, more than ready. But still he took his time with her, as if he would go on touching her forever. And the slow, exquisite torture was driving her over the edge.

She wanted—no, she needed him.

She lifted her hips off the mattress, silently seeking the fulfillment only he could give her.

''Not yet.'' He murmured the words as his fingertips continued their lazy exploration.

Her body melted back into the mattress on a soft, dreamy sigh. She'd never been touched like this before. So infinitely tenderly. So completely. His fingers skimmed over her, barely touching the flesh yet somehow branding her with fire, until her whole body was quivering, teetering on the brink. When he finally rose over her and slipped inside, she shattered.

Her eyes closed in delirious abandon and her hands clutched at the tightly bunched muscles in his shoulders, her fingernails digging into his flesh, as the orgasm ripped through her.

''Look at me, Nicole.''

She opened her eyes slowly, found his deep green gaze locked on her face.

''I want you to see that it's me loving you,'' he told her. ''I want you to see that I do love you.''

And she did. Just as she loved him. Always and forever.

Then he began to move inside her. Long, deep strokes that slowly drove her toward that brink again. She matched him, thrust for thrust, response for demand. Breaths mingling, bodies mating, hearts merging. And in perfect synchronicity, they leaped over the edge together.

The first rays of dawn were just starting to touch the sky when Nikki slipped from his bed the next morning. Colin got up with her, to kiss her goodbye, even though he'd be seeing her again in little more than an hour. He considered taking advantage of that hour to get some sleep, until the blinking light on the answering machine reminded him of Ian's call.

His agent had sounded excited about something when he'd called last night, but Colin had been too preoccupied with Nikki to care. He'd meant what he'd said—she was important to him. She and Carly were the most important part of his life. But now that Nikki was gone, he might as well find out what was going on with his agent.

He listened to the message, then picked up the phone to return the call.

"'Lo?" a groggy voice answered on the third ring.

"Ian, it's Colin."

"Christ, Colin." He heard a yawn, then another curse. "It's barely five o'clock in the morning here."

"You said to call as soon as I got the message. I just got the message—I'm calling."

"It's 5:00 a.m.," Ian grumbled again. "Which makes it—hell, it's too early to think. What time is it in Pennsylvania?"

"Six," Colin told him.

"What are you doing wandering in at—forget it," he decided. "I don't want to know."

Colin grinned. "I wasn't going to tell you anyway."

Ian grumbled some more.

"You had some news for me?" Colin prompted.

"I do. And it's better than what we hoped for."

"The Channel 12 deal?" Colin hoped so. Having a job that would keep him right here with Nikki and Carly was everything he wanted.

"Better," Ian said again. "The new owners want to renew your contract—on very favorable terms."

Excitement stirred in his gut. He didn't need to be told what a great opportunity it was: another chance to coach his team toward the Cup. "But—did I screw up my screen test? Did the brass at Channel 12 change their minds?''

He'd been told the job was practically a done deal, so long as he did well on the screen test, and so long as he wanted it. Which he did. Now more than ever.

"Colin—are you listening to me? This team will be a genuine contender next season."

There had been a time when that was all Colin wanted, when he'd have jumped to sign on the dotted line. So much had changed over the past few weeks.

"Okay," Ian said. "You're in shock. I can understand that. Just get your butt on a plane and get back here ASAP so we can finalize the details."

"You can't expect me to make a decision about this at six o'clock in the morning," Colin protested weakly. He knew he was being offered an incredible opportunity, but he wouldn't make any decisions without talking to Nikki first.

"I'll expect to hear from you later today," Ian said.

Nikki was just gulping down her second cup of coffee when Colin came to the door. She could tell right away that he had something on his mind. Something heavy. Uneasiness stirred in her heart as she wondered what could have happened since she'd left his bed to put that look of indecision in his eyes.

"Hi," she said softly.

"Morning, beautiful." He leaned over to brush a kiss on her lips. His arms came around her to hold her tight, but she could feel the tension in his body.

"Everything okay?" she asked.

He smiled, but she wasn't fooled.

"Sure," he agreed, and kissed her again. "I'll see you when you get home."

Nikki picked up her purse off the table and headed out the back door, wondering why he seemed so anxious to get rid of her. Whatever was on his mind was obviously not something he could talk about in five minutes. The uneasiness began to gnaw in earnest.

She tried to ignore her instincts. After all, they'd had an incredible weekend together. And last night, when he'd told her he loved her, her heart had practically spilled over with emotion.

She wanted to tell him that she loved him, too, but she knew that love wasn't always the answer. She *did* love him, but she still couldn't count on him staying in Fairweather, and she couldn't bear to think about him leaving.

Was that it? Was that why he'd seemed so distracted this morning? Had he already made plans to leave town again?

Damn you, Colin McIver, she cursed in the confines of her car as she drove toward the clinic. *Don't you dare walk out on me. Not now. Not when I'm starting to believe in you again.*

She pulled into an empty parking spot and turned off the ignition. She blinked away the tears that had sprung unbidden to her eyes. This is ridiculous, she chided herself. Yes, it was obvious that Colin had something on his mind. But he'd given her no indication about what it was, and she wasn't going to spend the day tying herself in knots over what it might or might not mean.

Still, that was exactly how she spent her day.

By the time she arrived back home that evening, her nerves were so tightly strung it amazed her that they didn't snap. Even Carly's jubilant greeting failed to ease the tension. Colin, she could tell, was as wound up as she.

"Are you going to tell me what's on your mind?" Nikki asked without preamble after they'd settled Carly into bed later that night.

Colin lowered himself onto the sofa, then tugged at

her hand to pull her down beside him. "That obvious, huh?"

"It's been driving me crazy all day," she admitted.

"I'm sorry."

But he didn't immediately offer an explanation. Instead, he covered her lips with his and kissed her. For those few moments, her mind cleared of all its wild imaginings, the tension in her body eased, and she felt secure in the comfort of his arms.

When she opened her eyes again, she found him staring at her, deeply, intently. "I love you, Nicole."

Her heart stuttered. Could it be so bad if he'd prefaced it like that?

Of course it could, the logical part of her brain snapped the reminder. Didn't he tell you he loved you when he walked out after that weekend five years ago?

"Please, Colin. Just tell me what's going on."

"I spoke to Ian Edwards today."

The name sounded vaguely familiar. Then she remembered—it was the name of the caller who'd left the message on Colin's answering machine last night.

"My agent," he explained. "I've been offered a new contract in Texas."

Nikki felt as though the bottom had dropped out of her stomach. This *was* the beginning of the end—the imminent moment she'd told herself that she'd been prepared for. But now that it was here, now that it was staring her in the face, she realized how completely unprepared she was.

She managed a tight smile. "You must be pleased."

"Ian couldn't tell me often enough what an opportunity it is."

"I'm sure it is," she agreed.

"I didn't tell him I'd take the job," Colin said.

A fragile blossom of hope sprouted somewhere deep

inside her. She trampled it viciously. "It's what you wanted," she reminded him.

He hesitated, then nodded. "Texas is a long way away."

She stood up, brushed her hands down the front of her slacks. As if maintaining outward composure and dignity could hold together the heart that was shattering into tiny little pieces. "You can visit Carly whenever you're in town."

"That wasn't quite the response I was hoping for," he told her.

She wouldn't break down in front of him; she wouldn't let him see how torn up she was inside. "What were you expecting?"

"I don't know. Anything but this…disinterest."

"I'm not disinterested. I'm happy for you. Really." And she was—thrilled for him, and mourning for herself and Carly, for everything they'd lost the minute he'd received that damn phone call. "When will you be leaving?"

He stared at her, long and hard, before responding. "Ian wants me back in Austin by the end of the week to finalize the terms of the contract, but I haven't made any plans."

"Have you told Carly?"

"Of course not. I wanted to talk to you and…" He faltered. "Dammit, Nicole. What about us?"

She managed a smile. "No strings, remember?"

"That was your rule," he said. "Maybe I want strings."

She shook her head. "I'm not going to wait for you, Colin. I can't."

"What if I asked you to come with me?"

Yes. She'd follow him to the ends of the earth if that was what he wanted, but she didn't think it was. It was just that he felt obligated to her now—to her and Carly.

She didn't want to hold him that way. Not five years ago, not now.

"I can't."

"You said if I'd asked you before, you would have gone with me."

She nodded slowly. "That was a long time ago. Everything was different then."

"Like what?" he demanded.

"Well, for one thing, we were married."

"So marry me."

Chapter 15

Nikki's heart jolted, her mind screamed yes. But she knew that one of them had to think about this rationally, and obviously it wasn't going to be Colin. It was so like him to spit out a proposal like that—reckless and impulsive, with no regard for the consequences.

"Marry me," he said again, then smiled.

"Don't be ridiculous, Colin."

His smile slipped, faded. "Why is it ridiculous?"

"Because you obviously haven't thought…" The words trailed off as he pulled a green velvet jeweler's box out of his pocket. He flipped open the lid, revealing a gorgeous thick gold band sparkling with channel-set diamonds.

"I *have* thought about this, Nicole."

She swallowed, determined to project an outward calm despite the chaos of emotions battling inside her heart. "Do you think I'm more likely to go with you if I have a ring on my finger?"

"I want us to be together."

She shook her head. "I can't marry you." *Not again.*

"Why not?"

Because I can't let my heart hope, and be broken, again. "Because I have to think about Carly. I have to do what's best for her."

Although she knew it was already too late to protect her daughter from the pain she'd feel when Colin left. It didn't matter that she'd never found out Colin was her father. Carly had bonded with him and his absence would leave a void in her life. All Nikki could do was be there for her.

"How could our getting married *not* be good for Carly?"

"She needs structure and stability in her life, and your work isn't conducive to either."

He tilted his head, studied her long and hard. "I never thought you were a coward, Nic. But you're hiding behind our daughter. You're using Carly as an excuse. I understand, because I've been there. I walked away from you once because I was terrified by how much I needed you. Now you're afraid to take a chance—"

"I think I've earned the right to be cautious." She crossed her arms over her chest. "You walked out on me once already."

"Is that what this is about?"

She paced across the living room, ignored the question.

"You said the past was forgotten," he reminded her, "but it's not. You can't forget what happened between us five years ago."

"How am I supposed to forget?" Nikki demanded. "That little girl sleeping upstairs is a daily reminder of our marriage, and the ease with which you walked away from it."

She paced to the other side of the room. "The irony of all of this is that I believed you had changed. I *wanted* to believe that you had."

From the bookcase, she picked up the large manila envelope Shaun had delivered a few days earlier. She tossed it onto the coffee table.

Colin picked it up, opened the flap. He pulled out the sheaf of papers, scanned through them. And tossed them back at her.

"We're not even on the same page." His words were tinged with sadness and resignation.

"I thought that was what you wanted. To have your paternal rights acknowledged, for Carly to know that you're her father."

"Not like this. Not all tied up in fancy words in some legal document that—dammit all—you went to my brother for." He gave a short, humorless laugh. "I didn't want a custody agreement. I wanted everything, Nic. You and me and Carly, together. A family."

"If you really wanted our relationship to work, you should have been honest with me."

He seemed genuinely baffled by her statement. "About what?"

"About whatever it is you've been hiding."

She caught it then, just a shadow of guilt that flickered quickly in his eyes before it was gone.

"I don't know what you mean."

She shook her head sadly. "Do you think I haven't noticed the way you always seem to be looking over your shoulder? The way you jump every time the phone rings? Not to mention your renewed friendship with Lieutenant Creighton."

Colin thought he'd been subtle. Nikki's comments certainly blew that theory out of the water.

"Dylan and I have been friends forever," he said, as if that simple statement explained everything.

"Something's going on, Colin. Something you've deliberately kept from me."

"I've been worried about some things," he admitted, "but—"

"What kind of things?"

"It's not important," he hedged.

"Damn it, Colin, it *is* important. This is exactly why our marriage fell apart five years ago—because we didn't talk about the things that mattered."

"I love you, Nic. That's the only thing that really matters."

"Love can't exist without trust," she said with finality.

He knew there was nothing he could say or do to change her mind, so he walked out.

He knew it was what Nikki expected him to do, and he hated to be predictable. He also knew he couldn't have stayed in that room with her one more minute without completely losing his temper. Or worse, completely falling apart.

How could she do this? How could she be so willing to throw away everything they had together?

It wasn't even the job, which surprised him. He'd thought it was what he wanted, but what he really wanted was to be with Nikki and Carly. He wanted his family. And it frustrated him to no end that Nikki refused to consider that possibility.

It frustrated him more to admit there was some validity to her accusations. He had been holding out on her, but only to protect her. He didn't want her to worry that he'd brought danger to her doorstep—he hadn't wanted to consider the possibility himself. So he'd withheld information, thinking it was for the best. Instead, his deception had created yet another barrier for them to overcome. A barrier they couldn't even begin to scale until he'd resolved the situation with Duncan Parnell.

Colin scrubbed his free hand over his face, wishing

that there was a simple solution to his dilemma. But once again, he was being forced to make a choice.

He laughed bitterly. Except that he didn't have a choice anymore. Nikki had taken the decision out of his hands when she'd told him to go. Obviously she didn't believe they had any kind of future together.

The phone was ringing when he stepped into his apartment. He didn't pick it up. It was probably just Ian calling again, and he wasn't in the mood to be harassed by his agent.

Despite her claim that she would have gone to Texas with him five years ago, she wouldn't even consider going now. Obviously she didn't love him as he loved her. The custody papers she'd given him had made it more than clear that he and Nikki were looking at their relationship from different perspectives. He wanted her forever. She, apparently, had a more limited time frame in mind.

The phone stopped ringing; the answering machine clicked on.

"Colin, it's Dylan. I've been trying to reach you at this number and your cell for the past hour and I keep getting this damn machine or your voice mail. If you get any one of the dozen messages I've left, call me right away."

Colin ignored the message and picked up his keys. The tone of Dylan's message nagged at him, but he wasn't in the mood to talk to anyone right now. He just wanted to drive for a while. Maybe he'd stop by the police station to see Dylan, but not yet. He needed some time and space to think first, the solitude of the road to help him come up with some answers.

The one thing he did know was that he wasn't giving up. No way in hell was he going to leave his wife and child.

He was walking out to his Jeep when another vehicle

pulled into the driveway with a squeal of tires, blocking him in. Dylan Creighton bounded out of the car toward him.

"Why the hell don't you answer your phone, McIver?" The detective's tone conveyed both anger and relief.

"I was on my way out."

"Then you're damn lucky we got here when we did."

It wasn't until Dylan's "we" that Colin noticed the other officer who had stepped out of the vehicle and was now donning something that looked like an armored space suit. "Who's that?"

"Mark Wallace, otherwise known as the Fairweather Bomb Squad."

"Bomb Squad?" Colin frowned. "What are you talking about?"

"Just give me your keys," Dylan instructed.

Colin handed them over.

"Give *me* the keys," Mark said, zipping up the front of his suit. He held out a hand, and Dylan relinquished the keys.

"Is someone going to tell me what the hell's going on?" Colin demanded.

"Maybe nothing," Dylan told him, as Mark unlocked the Jeep, then released the latch on the hood. "But we're about to find out."

"Stay away from the vehicle," Mark said.

Colin ignored the order and moved closer to peer over the bomb technician's shoulder. He sucked in a breath as he spotted what appeared to be a blob of white modeling clay with a series of wires protruding from it attached to his engine.

He retreated quickly. Although he'd never seen anything like it, he'd be willing to bet both his Stanley Cup rings that it was a bomb.

"Come on," Dylan said, taking Colin's arm to steer

him farther away from the vehicle. "Let's get out of the way so Mark can do his job."

"How did you know it was there?" Colin asked.

Dylan blew out a breath. "Sheer dumb luck," he admitted. "I have a contact, someone who sometimes passes along information to me."

"A snitch?"

"He objects to that term, but yeah. Anyway, he heard from someone else that a local dealer of explosives had recently sold a small quantity of C-4. He was apprehensive about dealing with an out-of-towner, but the opportunity was too good to pass up. When the client picked up the merchandise, he hinted about his plans, about the high-profile case he was working on."

"And you concluded I was the target from that?"

"It was a leap," Dylan admitted, "but a logical one, considering the attempts on your life in Texas and Maryland had both involved bombs."

Colin leaned back against the side of the house. Dylan was right. It was sheer dumb luck that he'd been alerted about the bomb. Sheer dumb luck that Colin was still alive.

After only a few minutes, Mark stepped away from the Jeep, holding the device in his hand.

"Isn't that dangerous?" Colin asked.

"Not now," the detective told him, sliding the device into a clear evidence bag. "This kind of bomb requires a charge in order to detonate. It was attached to the vehicle's starter box, designed to go off when the current from the starter hits the electrical ignition switch."

"You mean as soon as I turned the key..."

"...it would have set off the bomb," Mark finished for him.

Colin glanced from his Jeep to the house, where Nikki and his daughter lived. If the bomb had detonated— He hadn't even completed the thought before another, even more horrifying one, struck: what if Nikki and Carly had been in the Jeep with him?

The possibility staggered him. He'd come to Fairweather to hide out, and in doing so he'd brought danger to the door of his ex-wife and their child. So long as he remained in town, both Nikki and Carly were in jeopardy.

"We'll have someone come out to tow the vehicle to the crime lab for further testing," Mark said.

Colin just nodded.

"Are you okay?" Dylan asked.

Colin managed to laugh. "I'm alive. I guess I should at least be grateful for that."

"We'll find who did this," Dylan promised him. "We already know where the explosive came from, which is a huge break in a case like this."

"Your friend said the guy was a professional. Finding him won't end this." Especially not with Parnell still at large.

"It's the first step."

Colin wished he could believe it, but the nightmare had become far too real, the killer had struck too close to home. "I'm going back to Texas tomorrow," he decided.

"Why?"

"I came to Fairweather because I believed I could be safe here. I'm not—and neither are Nikki or Carly, not as long as I'm around." He knew that Dylan, better than anyone, would understand the grief and guilt that would consume him if anything happened to his family.

Dylan nodded. "I'll send a copy of my report to Detective Brock and keep him apprised of new developments on this end."

"Thanks." He shook Dylan's hand. "For everything."

Colin returned to his apartment and grabbed a beer out of the refrigerator, wishing like hell he had something stronger to steel his frayed nerves. He wanted nothing more than to get drunk—to forget how close he'd come to putting his key in the ignition and sending his sorry soul to its fateful end.

He twisted the top off the bottle and drank deeply. He had only one thing to do now: book a ticket out of this town. It wasn't a task that he looked forward to with any enthusiasm, but it was a necessary one.

He'd take the first flight available tomorrow afternoon, even if it got him to Texas via Alaska. All that mattered was getting away, keeping Nikki and Carly safe.

He would have to tell them he was going, and he had no idea how he was going to do that. Not that the words really mattered. Nothing he could say would make it any easier.

"I'm going back to Texas."

Nikki had almost convinced herself she was prepared for such an announcement, until Colin actually said the words aloud.

"When?"

"Today. After we talked last night…" He shrugged, as if the words he sought eluded him. "I just think it's better this way."

It was Nikki's turn to nod. This was what she'd expected. Why, then, did she feel an inexplicable sense of loss?

"You were right," he told her. "The coaching job is just too good an opportunity to pass up."

Because after he'd left last night she'd spent the better part of the long, lonely evening reconsidering his offer. Because although she knew it would be a gamble, she'd decided they did deserve a second chance. And because she'd promised herself that if he asked her again to go to Texas with him, she'd say "yes."

But it didn't seem as though he had any intention of

asking her again. So she swallowed her pride and finally said, "Did you still want me and Carly to go with you?"

He seemed startled by the question, almost panicked by the thought. The reaction might have amused her, if it hadn't hurt so much.

"No," he said. "Your objections were valid—and my proposal was an impulse. You and Carly have a life here."

"And your life is in Texas."

"I can't pass up this opportunity."

It was difficult to swallow around the sudden tightness in her throat. "Have you told Carly?"

Something—pain? regret?—flashed in his eyes. "Yeah. And I've already contacted her day camp, to register her for the rest of the summer."

"Oh. Good." He obviously wasn't wasting any time. Well, that was probably for the best—there was no point in delaying the inevitable.

"Maybe this time we could say a proper goodbye," he suggested.

He laid his hands on her shoulders, stroked them down her arms. The simple touch sent the blood racing through her veins.

"Just one last kiss, Nicole."

One kiss. She couldn't refuse his request, couldn't refuse herself this last opportunity for closure.

She tilted her face toward him. His lips brushed against hers. The touch was soft as a whisper, and somehow more powerful than anything she'd ever experienced.

He laid his palms against hers, laced their fingers together. He kissed her for what seemed like forever, with such infinite gentleness that it brought tears to her eyes.

And she responded with everything in her heart, able to hold nothing back. She'd never been able to hold back with Colin. Once again, she'd given him everything she had, everything she was, and she'd been left with nothing.

She grasped at the thought, but it slipped away, and her mind went completely blank as his tongue swept along the seam of her lips. She opened for him, met him eagerly, conscious only of the multitude of sensations evoked by his kiss. Of the feeling that she and Colin were inextricably linked—hand to hand, heart to heart. Forever.

Except this wasn't forever.

This was goodbye.

As if the thought had been transmitted from her subconscious to his, Colin slowly eased his lips from hers.

She leaned her forehead against his chest and concentrated on breathing. She could feel the heavy pounding of his heart. Or was it her own?

Taking another breath, she drew back and found that her knees were still unsteady but able to support her weight. Then she looked at him, and the depth of emotion in his eyes stunned her.

"I—"

She didn't know what he'd planned to say, only that she was certain she didn't want to hear it. She shook her head fiercely to halt his words and blinked against the tears that threatened. He'd made the decision to leave; there was no point in saying anything more.

"Good luck, Colin." Her voice wasn't as steady as she'd hoped.

Colin exhaled, but squeezed her hands gently before releasing them. "Goodbye, Nic."

Colin had booked a one-way ticket in his own name direct to Texas. Whoever the bastard was that was after him, he wanted him to follow this time. He wanted him as far away from Fairweather and Nikki and Carly as was possible.

He leaned back against the headrest and closed his eyes, unable to fathom how much he missed them already.

He never would have thought it was possible to love someone as quickly, as fiercely, as he loved his little girl. But from the first moment he'd set eyes on her, he'd felt a connection between them. A bond of blood that would never be broken—even if they were separated by more than a thousand miles.

His heart broke a little more with each mile as the plane took him farther and farther away from her. Carly had lived the first four-and-a-half years of her life without him; she didn't need him. But he wanted to believe she'd miss him, just a little.

Colin's throat tightened. He didn't want to be the kind of father who sent gifts for birthdays and other special occasions. He didn't want to talk to his daughter once a week over a long-distance phone line. He wanted to be there for her, every day. But he would stay away from her and be glad of the distance if it was the only way to keep her safe.

It might not be such a big adjustment for Carly, anyway. After all, it wasn't as if she was losing her father. She'd understand that "Uncle Colin" had to go away for a new job. And maybe, one day, Nikki would find someone to be the kind of husband she wanted, the kind of father Carly deserved.

He wouldn't have thought it was possible, but the knife that had plunged into his heart when he'd said goodbye to his family dug even deeper, twisted painfully. He couldn't stand the idea of Carly calling anyone else "Daddy," even if she'd never used that title for him. He didn't want to even imagine Nikki with another man.

God, he would do anything to erase the stark pain he'd seen in Nikki's eyes—pain he'd caused. He knew she thought he was leaving because he didn't love her enough to stay. The truth was that he loved her too much.

He knew he'd done the right thing by leaving Fairweather, but his conviction didn't make the emptiness any more bearable.

Needing a diversion, he called Ian from the skyphone on the plane. With his agent's help, maybe he could finally put an end to the games.

"I'm on my way back," he said when Ian answered the phone.

His agent's relief was palpable. "I'm glad you finally came to your senses."

Colin didn't bother to dispute the point. "I want you to contact the media."

"Why?"

"I want it known that the Tornadoes intend to re-sign me, that I'm returning to finalize negotiations."

"I'm sure it will be in the news after the contract is signed."

"I want it on the news *today*."

"All right," Ian relented after only a brief hesitation.

Colin ended the call with a grim sense of purpose.

Come and get me, you bastard.

Chapter 16

When Arden came home from work that afternoon, Nikki was sitting alone in the living room. She wasn't crying. She'd shed more than enough tears over Colin McIver to last a dozen lifetimes, and she refused to cry anymore. There was nothing left inside her, anyway. Colin had been gone for three hours, and her heart was as empty as the apartment downstairs.

"What happened?" Arden asked, concern in her voice. "Is something wrong with Carly?"

Nikki shook her head. "Carly's fine. She's upstairs playing."

"What's wrong?"

Her throat tightened and traitorous tears burned behind her eyes. "Colin's gone."

Arden sat down on the sofa beside her. "Gone where?"

"He went back to Texas today."

"Why?"

"His agent called. He's going to be coaching in Austin this year."

"Colin's agent is coaching in Austin?"

Nikki managed a slight smile. "No. Colin's going to be coaching in Austin."

"Oh." There was a wealth of understanding, and empathy, in that single word.

"Yeah."

Arden put her slender arms around Nikki's shoulders. "I'm so sorry, Nic. I thought…well, it doesn't matter what I thought." She held her tighter.

"I should have been prepared for this," Nikki said, her voice sounding strangely hollow to her own ears. "I thought I *was* prepared for this. But when he drove away…"

Her only consolation was that he hadn't looked back, hadn't seen her standing at the window watching him leave. Again.

"I hate him for doing this to you. Again."

"Me, too." But she could—she would—hold it together. She had more important things to think about than her own disappointment. "I hate even more to think about how Carly will be affected by this."

"She's a kid, she'll bounce back." Arden's deep brown eyes probed gently. "I'm more worried about you."

"I'm okay."

"You don't look okay."

"Thanks," Nikki said dryly.

"You miss him already, don't you?"

"Maybe."

Definitely.

She'd thought she'd protected her heart this time. As if by not speaking the words out loud she could prevent herself from loving him. She knew now that wasn't possible. She did love Colin. It was possible she'd never stopped loving him.

"Did you tell him?" Arden asked, somehow following her cousin's internal monologue.

She shook her head.

"I think you should," her cousin urged. "If he knew how you felt about him—"

"It's too late."

"I don't believe that. A man doesn't look at a woman the way Colin looks at you unless he has some pretty strong feelings."

"Not strong enough, obviously." She was helpless to prevent the bitterness from creeping into her voice. He'd told her he loved her, but when it came right down to it, he loved hockey more.

"I must have been a victim of temporary insanity," Nikki confessed. "I promised myself I wouldn't get involved with him, and I did anyway. But I managed to justify it to myself. Spending time together, sharing laughs, having a consensual sexual relationship—there was no harm in any of that so long as I didn't fall in love with him."

"But you did," Arden said softly.

"Yeah." She swiped at the tears that spilled onto her cheeks. "I am such an idiot."

"Love makes people do crazy things."

"I didn't expect him to stay for me," she said. "Not really. But I thought…I hoped…that he might…maybe…for Carly."

"Does she know he's gone?"

Nikki nodded.

"How's she handling it?"

"She seems okay. So far, anyway. We'll see what happens when she has to go to day camp tomorrow morning."

"Just take it one day at a time," Arden advised.

Nikki nodded, knowing that was all she could hope to do.

She forced aside the regret and moved on with her day. Her heart might be feeling a little battered and bruised, but there were still things that needed to be done.

She was putting laundry away in Carly's dresser when she heard the crinkle of paper. She lifted the stack of T-shirts and found a selection of crudely cut newspaper clippings. The headline on the top was all too familiar to her. "Hometown Hero Returns." Beneath was a file photo of Colin from his hockey days, and a silver framed photograph of Nikki and Colin on their wedding day.

Nikki had almost forgotten that she'd given Carly the picture. Most of the mementos of her ill-fated marriage had been tucked away in boxes in the attic, but when Carly had first starting asking questions about her father, she'd given her the picture. She'd wanted Carly to know that there was a time when her parents had been in love.

Beneath the photo was a drawing that Carly had done herself. Based on the brown hair and the green eyes, Nikki guessed that it was a picture of Colin. Except that he was wearing a pink cape and had a large *D* emblazoned on his chest.

She didn't even want to think about what kind of fantasies her highly imaginative daughter had devised where Colin was concerned. Did she think that Colin was some kind of hero? Where would she ever get such an idea?

Knowing that she had no choice but to destroy Carly's illusions, Nikki picked up the handful of items and headed downstairs to find her daughter.

"What is this, Carly?"

Carly's eyes widened when she saw the picture in her mother's hand, but she didn't respond to the question.

"Is this a picture of Uncle Colin?" Nikki asked gently.

Chewing on her bottom lip, Carly tapped the toe of her sneaker against the leg of the table. With obvious reluctance, she nodded. "But please, Mommy, don't tell anybody."

"Don't tell anyone what?"

Carly glanced around, as if to ensure that no one else was within hearing distance. The room was empty, but still she pitched her voice to a whisper. "That Daddy's a superhero."

Daddy? Superhero? She didn't know which part of her daughter's matter-of-fact statement disturbed her more. Did Carly know that Colin was her father, or was she only wishing that he could be? And how did superhero status figure into the equation?

"You have to promise not to tell anyone, Mommy." Carly sounded frantic now.

Nikki sighed and pulled her daughter into her lap, desperately trying to unravel the mystery. "Uncle Colin's not a superhero," she explained patiently, hoping that she could ignore the "daddy" issue for even a few minutes longer.

Carly nodded her head. "I know. Uncle Colin's like Kitty. But Daddy's like Cosmic Cat." She was whispering again.

If Nikki had been confused before, now she was completely baffled. Kitty? Cosmic Cat? What did any of this have to do with Colin?

"I don't understand," Nikki said, but then the newspaper clipping caught her eye again. The words "Hometown Hero" blazed from the headlines, words her daughter, with her rudimentary reading skills, had somehow managed to decipher. Suddenly Nikki was all too afraid she did understand.

"Every superhero has a secret identity," Carly explained. "Then the bad guys can't find them. That's why Daddy was pretending to be Uncle Colin."

Nikki cringed inwardly, wondering why she'd ever thought it was a good idea to keep the truth from their daughter. Wondering if it was possible to undo the damage she'd done.

"You know that Uncle Colin is your daddy?"

Carly nodded. "But he was in disguise."

It was time, Nikki decided, to cut through all the lies and illusions with the unvarnished truth. Her daughter deserved no less.

"Uncle Colin is your daddy," Nikki confirmed, feeling as if an enormous weight had been lifted off her chest as she spoke the words. "But he's not a superhero. He doesn't fight crime or bad guys, and he doesn't wear a pink cape." Or if he did, she'd never seen it. But that wasn't the point, anyway.

"He can't fly without a cape," Carly said.

"He can't fly without a pilot," she responded dryly.

"He told me he was flying to Texas."

"He was. He was going to Texas in an airplane. Like when we went on an airplane to visit Grandma in California last year. Do you remember?"

"Oh." Then, "But he told me he was going away for a job."

"That doesn't make him a superhero," she said gently.

"Then why can't he work here?" Carly's lower lip jutted out, her eyes filled with tears. "Why did he have to go away?"

Nikki felt her own eyes stinging. This was what she'd wanted to avoid, the reason she hadn't wanted Carly to know that Colin was her father. Now she recognized the folly in that assumption. Carly loved Colin, and because she loved him, she missed him.

She blinked away the moisture. "The kind of job your daddy wants to do isn't available around here."

"Can't he get another job?"

She sighed. Of course he could, but how could she explain the complexity of the situation to an almost-five-year-old?

"Do you remember the other day, when you wanted to go to the park?" she asked. "I told you that we could go, but only after you'd picked up all of your toys."

Carly's forehead puckered into a frown, but she nodded.

"Well, if Daddy got a job here, it would be like having to pick up toys all the time. The job he's going to in Texas is like being able to play at the park."

Carly considered the explanation, then she sighed. "I'd go to Texas, too."

Nikki smiled and wrapped her arms around her daughter, holding her close. "I know you would, honey."

Carly was silent for a long moment, and Nikki breathed a sigh of relief, mistakenly assuming that she'd survived the worst of her daughter's interrogation.

"I want to go to Texas. I want to be with Daddy."

The words squeezed Nikki's heart like a fist, and she couldn't help but feel rejected. First by Colin, who had once again chosen not to stay with her. And by their daughter, whose statement confirmed her worst fears: Carly would rather be with Colin than with her.

"Why can't we go to Texas?" Carly asked.

The "we" in the question soothed a little. Maybe Carly wasn't ready to abandon her mother, after all. Still, Nikki felt a pang of regret that she couldn't give her daughter the one thing she knew she really wanted: her mommy *and* her daddy. A real family.

"We can't go to Texas because we live here. Mommy has a job here, and you're going back to school in September."

Silence descended again as Carly seemed to digest this information. "Was it because of the ring?" she asked after a long moment, the question spoken in a hesitant whisper.

"What ring?" But she was all too afraid she knew

what Carly was going to say. And she damned Colin to hell for ever having given their daughter false hope.

"The ring Uncle—Daddy bought for you. Didn't you like it?" Carly's green eyes filled with tears again. "I picked out one with lots of pretty stones."

If her heart hadn't been breaking all over again for her little girl, Nikki might have smiled. Only a child would describe about three carats worth of diamonds as "pretty stones." She swallowed the lump in her throat. "It was a beautiful ring."

"Then why didn't you want to marry him?"

"It's complicated, honey." She winced at her own words, but she didn't know how to make her daughter understand something she wasn't sure she understood herself.

Her reasons had seemed valid at the time Colin had proposed. Now that he was gone, they were less clear. She'd wanted him to stay. She'd wanted him to love her enough to choose her. But he'd chosen to go.

Or maybe she'd been too rigid in her expectations. Yes, he'd wanted to go, but he'd asked her to go with him. He'd wanted to marry her again, to give them a chance to be a real family. Wasn't that proof enough that he loved her?

He could have turned down the job, a nagging voice reminded her.

But why would he? She'd as much as told him to go. She'd given him no reason to believe that she wanted him to stay. She'd never even told him that she loved him.

Would it have made a difference?

She didn't really know. But she did know that she couldn't spend the rest of her life—and Carly's—wondering what might have been if only she'd had the courage to tell him how she felt, what she wanted.

She was reaching for the phone when the doorbell rang.

* * *

Dylan Creighton was almost the last person Nikki expected to find on her front porch, but she forced a smile for the detective. If she could pretend her heart wasn't broken, maybe it really wouldn't be.

"If you're looking for Colin, you've missed him," she told Dylan. "He went back to Texas today."

"I know. I came to see you."

"Oh." She stepped away from the door. "Did you want to come in?"

He stepped into the foyer.

"Can I get you something to drink—coffee or a beer or—"

"No, thanks," he interrupted.

"Are you here in an official capacity?" she finally asked.

He shook his head. "I'm here as a friend. As a favor to Colin, although I'm not sure he'll agree."

Now she was really confused. "Does Colin know you're here?"

"No. But I thought you had a right to know."

"Know what?" she asked, just a little impatiently.

"Why Colin went back to Texas."

"To renew his coaching contract."

"No. He left because we found a bomb wired to the starter in his Jeep last night," Dylan explained.

Nikki sank into a chair, stunned. "I don't understand."

"I'm walking a fine line here," he admitted. "Revealing information about an ongoing investigation. But since the incident occurred on your property, I figured you had a right to know. And I didn't think Colin would tell you."

"He didn't," Nikki admitted. She folded her hands in her lap, trying to assimilate everything he'd told her. "I knew about the threats and the explosion in his condo, but Colin told me an arrest had been made.''

''It had,'' Dylan agreed. ''But the police suspected right from the beginning that the bomb was planted by a hired killer. The second bombing in Baltimore confirmed it.''

''Baltimore?''

He winced. ''He didn't tell you about that?''

She shook her head.

''Then let's pretend I didn't tell you, either.''

''You said you were here because I had a right to know,'' she reminded him.

''And I wanted you to know we've got a suspect in custody,'' he said, neatly sidestepping her demand.

''Oh.'' She exhaled a shaky breath. ''Well, that's good news, I guess.''

''He's already indicated his willingness to make a deal—to give us the name of the man who hired him. The D.A.'s office is just working out the details with his lawyer.''

Nikki sat alone for a long time after Dylan had gone, trying to assimilate the information he'd given her and sort out the chaotic emotions churning in her. She was hurt and angry that Colin hadn't trusted her enough to tell her about the other attempts on his life. Relieved that the man who'd been trying to kill him was in jail. And confused about his motivation for returning to Texas.

Had he left to accept the coaching job, as he'd told her? Or had he used that as an excuse in order to protect her and Carly?

The only way to know for sure, she decided, was to ask Colin.

Duncan Parnell sat slumped in a borrowed car, parked outside the exclusive condominium complex that was home to upper-class professional couples and corporate

CEOs and his former hockey coach. He'd been waiting for more than an hour already—since he'd heard about McIver's return on the midday news. He was prepared to wait as long as he had to. He wasn't prepared to let McIver get away with ruining his life.

He was probably inside now, meeting with his agent to discuss the new contract. That only pissed him off further. McIver was the one who had blown their chances at the Cup, yet he was the one getting the offers. Duncan Parnell had gone the extra mile, and now he was a fugitive from the law.

He saw the taxi pull up at the front door, paid no attention to it until he saw the woman emerge. He recognized her immediately. As soon as Boomer had mentioned that McIver was hanging out in Fairweather, Pennsylvania, with a woman and kid, Duncan had done some research. He hadn't found anything on the kid, but he'd found pictures of McIver and this woman in some old newspapers. She was Nikki Gordon McIver, McIver's ex-wife.

He got out of his car just in time to hear the doorman directing her to the fifteenth floor.

"Mrs. McIver." He had to hurry to catch up with her and almost stumbled with the pain.

She turned, a half smile curving her lips. "I haven't been called that in a long time."

He forced a smile, offered a hand. "Duncan Parnell," he said. "If you're looking for Coach, you just missed him."

Her smile faded. "Oh."

"He had a meeting at the rink. I just stopped by to pick up some papers he forgot." Duncan held up the manila envelope he was carrying.

"Do you know how long he'll be?"

"Who knows? Sometimes these executive meetings are over quickly, sometimes they can go on for hours."

He paused for a moment. "I'm on my way over there, if you wanted to catch a lift."

She hesitated. "He isn't expecting me," she admitted.

"Then I'm sure he'll be pleasantly surprised." He smiled again. His sister had always said he was a real charmer when he wanted to be.

"Are you sure you don't mind?"

"Of course not. As I said, I'm going that way myself."

"Thanks."

She followed him to his car.

Chapter 17

"I don't understand why you're hesitating." Ian sounded genuinely confused. "The offer is more than fair."

Colin nodded his agreement absently. The pen was in his hand, poised over the contract. All he had to do was sign his name and his life would once again have purpose. The dotted line beckoned, tempted. Or tried to. In his heart, he just wasn't ready to make this commitment.

He dropped the pen and pushed away from the table. He caught a glimpse of the scowl that marred his agent's face, but he ignored it as he strode over to the window to stare unseeingly at the city spread out below.

He'd spoken on the phone to both Dylan Creighton and Detective Brock before Ian had shown up. Dylan had even faxed him a picture of the suspect, and Colin had recognized him immediately as the solitary man from the zoo. He broke out in a cold sweat just thinking about how close the killer had been to Nikki and Carly. But

Louis "Boomer" Parker was behind bars now, and Nikki and Carly were safe.

Dylan had also told him that, in exchange for a deal, Boomer had provided proof of Duncan Parnell's involvement. Colin was both surprised and disappointed by the confirmation that it was Parnell who had set this whole thing in motion. He never would have guessed the young man harbored so much hatred, resentment and bitterness that he would have gone to such extreme measures to seek his revenge. All because of a game.

He could almost hear his father's voice speaking those words. Words that would have infuriated Colin in the past now seemed so fitting.

Once upon a time, hockey had been his life. That time had passed. He still loved the game and everything it entailed, but it was no longer the center of his world.

Unfortunately, it was all he had left. He'd severed ties with Nikki and Carly to come back here. He'd made Nikki believe that he'd left her because he couldn't give up the chance to coach again. Would she ever believe otherwise?

"Are you going to tell me why you seem to be on the brink of throwing away your future?" Ian asked.

Colin turned away from the window, scanned the familiar surroundings of his apartment. It was a spectacular apartment—spacious, inviting. The decor was tasteful if somewhat bland. Everything in cool neutral tones of cream and taupe. Nothing at all like the splashes of color that permeated Nikki's house.

The carpet was plush beneath his feet, spotless. No grape juice had ever been spilled on it, no dirty sneakers had trod upon it. The sofa—a cream and tan stripe—was as comfortable as it had been expensive, the glossy table was some kind of antique, and the blown-glass bowl at its center was the work of some up-and-coming local artisan.

Everything in this apartment was what he'd always thought he wanted, and yet it had never felt like home. Home, he now realized, was wherever Nikki and Carly were.

He missed them unbearably.

Moving back to the window, he thought of Carly, with her glowing eyes and infectious laughter. All he had to do was close his eyes and he could breathe in the soft, baby-powder scent that would forever remind him of her. He could almost feel her little arms wrapped around him, the slight weight of her sleepy head on his shoulder. And he'd never forget the disappointment in her eyes when he'd told her he was going away.

He blinked the memory away along with the moisture stinging his eyes. Carly would be okay, she had Nikki.

Nikki.

He missed her as much as he missed Carly. He missed her smile, her touch, her taste. He missed everything about her.

He'd made so many mistakes where she was concerned, and he'd missed so much by turning away from her five years earlier. He'd hurt her when he'd left her—alone and pregnant. It wasn't surprising that she still didn't trust him.

And now he'd hurt her again—deliberately this time—by turning away from her and returning to Texas. How could he expect that she'd ever give him another chance? How could he ask her to trust that he wouldn't walk out on her when he'd done exactly that twice already?

He watched a cab pull up to the curb, did a double take when he saw the woman emerge. Nikki?

He shook his head. Of course it wasn't Nikki. She was in Fairweather and he was on the fifteenth floor looking down on the sidewalk. From this vantage point, he could imagine that any blond woman was Nikki.

"Colin?"

He forgot about the woman on the sidewalk and turned back to his agent, casting another cursory glance around the room. By all outward appearances, he was a man to be envied. The truth was a different matter. Job or no job, without Nikki and Carly, his life was empty. Meaningless.

And that was why he had no intention of hanging around in Texas when they were in Fairweather.

"I'm not going to sign, Ian."

"What?"

Colin couldn't blame him for being shocked. He was a little stunned himself, but now that he'd spoken the words aloud, he felt infinitely better.

"I'm sorry. I know you worked hard to put this deal together, but—"

"You asked me to put this deal together," Ian reminded him. "You told me to contact the press, to announce your intention to sign."

"I had my reasons for that," Colin said. "But this contract isn't going to happen?"

"Why the hell not?"

Colin only smiled, at last secure in the knowledge of what he wanted. And determined to get it.

"Please, Colin. Tell me you're not throwing your future away over a woman."

Colin shook his head, but his smile widened. "Not just *a* woman," he said. "Two very special women."

"This is it," Duncan said, pulling into a mostly vacant parking lot behind what he'd called the "rink." Nikki glanced around at what was, in reality, a huge coliseum-style sports complex that seated upward of fifteen thousand hockey fans.

"Nice," she said, eyeing the building.

"You never been here before?" he asked.

"I've never even been to Texas before," she admitted.

"If I'd known that, I would have pointed out some of the sights along the way."

She smiled as she followed him through the lobby. He reminded her so much of Colin when they'd first met. All cocky self-confidence and boyish charm.

They walked up several flights of wide stairs and past a series of concession stands, finally arriving at a closed door.

"This is Coach's office," he said, sliding a key into the lock.

Nikki frowned. "Isn't he here?"

"The meeting is down the hall," Duncan explained. "But I thought you'd be more comfortable waiting in here until he's done."

"Okay."

She didn't think anything was amiss until he closed the door behind them and locked it.

Nikki's heart stopped for a beat, then began to pound slowly, laboriously, against her ribs. "What's going on, Duncan?"

He turned. His mouth was no longer smiling, and his eyes were no longer warm. "We're going to wait here."

"Why did you lock the door?"

"Because this is a private party—by invitation only." Then he reached into the back of his pants and pulled out a gun. "This," he said, gesturing with the weapon, "is your personal invitation."

Nikki was at a complete loss for what to say or do. The moment he pulled out that gun, her brain had simply frozen.

Duncan gestured toward the chair behind the desk. "Sit."

She sat.

She tried to think of something to say, figure out some way to reason with him, but his waving of the gun made her nervous. Even if he didn't intend to shoot her, the gun could discharge accidentally, and a stray bullet could kill her as effectively as a well-aimed one.

"Pick up the phone," Parnell said.

Again she did as she was told.

"Call him."

"Who?"

Duncan glared at her. "McIver."

She reached a trembling hand toward the receiver.

"No." Duncan's hand came down on top of hers. "Use the speakerphone," he instructed, then grinned. "I want to hear the panic in his voice when he realizes you're with me."

"What are you planning to do?"

"We can discuss that later," he said dismissively. "After you've made the call."

He pressed the button for the speakerphone, and the sound of a dial tone filled the air.

"I only know his cell-phone number."

"Then try that one first," he said, gesturing for her to do so.

She dialed carefully, her finger shaking so badly she was afraid she'd misdial, and afraid of the wrath that might be directed toward her for such a mistake.

Colin answered on the second ring.

"Hello?"

The relief of hearing his voice was almost overwhelming. Tears sprang to her eyes and she had to bite down on her lip to keep from sobbing.

"Hello?" he said again, just a little impatiently.

Duncan nudged her shoulder with the muzzle of the gun. "Talk," he muttered the order in her ear. "The idea is for him to know that you're here."

Nikki swallowed the emotions that clogged her throat. "C-Colin, it's me."

"Nicole." She could hear the pleasure in his voice. "I've been trying to get in touch with you. I—"

"Colin, wait."

He must have sensed the tension in her voice. "What's wrong? Is it Carly?"

"No—"

"Hey, Coach." Duncan interrupted, his tone filled with false cheerfulness.

There was a brief second of tense silence. "What the hell's going on, Parnell?"

"I'm just taking some time to get acquainted with your pretty ex-wife."

"Where are you?"

"We're at the arena, in your old office, in fact."

"I'm on my way."

Duncan grinned. "You have ten minutes. I'm not sure my finger will be able to hold steady on the trigger any longer than that."

Ten minutes.

Nikki closed her eyes, silently praying that Colin would make it on time. But even if he did, she didn't know what Duncan Parnell's next move would be. Would he kill her anyway? Did he plan to kill Colin?

Her eyes flew open as he nudged her chair aside and began rummaging through the desk drawers. Although his attention seemed focused on his search, the gun remained pointed in her general direction.

"Aha," he said at last, and held up a roll of duct tape.

Nikki wasn't as thrilled with his find, especially when he began wrapping the tape around her ankles.

"Is that really necessary?" she asked.

"I can't take any chances that you'll try to get away," he said, wrapping the tape so tightly it dug into her flesh. "Put your hands on the arms of the chair."

She considered refusing. Meek submission wasn't in her nature, but she thought of her daughter waiting for her in Fairweather, and of Colin, and the sacrifices he'd already made for them. Accepting that the tape was a lot less lethal than the bullets in the gun, she did as he instructed.

"It was you, wasn't it?" she asked.

"What was me?"

"You hired someone to kill Colin."

"If you want something done right, you've got to do it yourself."

She wasn't sure if his statement was supposed to be a confirmation or denial, but the grim purpose of his tone convinced Nikki that this man was her ex-husband's stalker. And she'd walked right into his trap.

He'd introduced himself as one of Colin's players. She'd never even suspected that he could be the one who'd tried to kill Colin. But why would she? Colin had never told her the man's name, and she'd believed he was in jail.

"Why are you doing this?" she finally ventured to ask.

"Because my life is ruined," he told her, tearing the last piece of tape from the roll. "And it's all McIver's fault."

"Because he scratched you from the lineup?"

"Right before the play-offs," he said, as if that explained everything. "Everyone knows that's the real reason we never made it to the Cup."

"He must have had a reason." She was desperate to keep him talking, desperately praying for a solution out of this situation she'd somehow managed to get herself in.

"Because he was jealous of my success."

"Colin was a pretty good hockey player in his day," Nikki said.

"Pretty good," Duncan scoffed. "After only my second year, the press were making comparisons to Gretzky."

"What happened?"

"Damn car accident. Buggered up my back pretty good. I lost five weeks in the middle of the season."

"Must have been difficult to get back into the rhythm of things after so much time off," Nikki said sympathetically.

"Maybe for someone else," he said. "Coach said I needed to take some time—get myself back together. Dammit, I was together. There was no one more together than me."

"Did you talk to him about this?"

"Talk? Hell, I *begged* him to let me play." He shook his head. "He took away my shot at the Cup."

"You're young," she appeased. "You'll have other years, other chances."

"Maybe. Maybe not. My contract is up this year, and no one's expressed any interest in signing me. If he'd let me play, I would have shown them what I could do. This was *my* year, and he took that away from me."

She was no longer convinced that talking was a good idea. The more Duncan ranted, the more agitated he became. But there was just one more question she needed to ask. "What does any of this have to do with me?"

He shrugged philosophically. "Wrong place at the wrong time, sweetheart. I was waiting for McIver and you showed up instead. And now I'm going to make him suffer, like he made me suffer."

Colin was at the arena in seven minutes, somehow managing to dial Detective Brock while en route. He didn't bother to park his car but left it in front of the building, then took another minute and a half to race up the stairs toward the executive offices.

He tried the knob, but it wouldn't turn. He banged his fist on the door. "Open up, Parnell."

He heard a click as the bolt was released. Detective

Brock's warning to wait for the police echoed dimly in the back of his mind.

Parnell had Nikki inside—Colin wasn't waiting for anything.

He pushed open the door and stepped into the room. And directly into the line of fire.

Parnell glanced idly at the clock on the wall. "You made pretty good time, Coach. You must have been...motivated."

Colin ignored the comment, his attention focused on Nikki. She'd been tied to his chair, but other than the restraints at her wrists, she looked unharmed. Terrified, but unharmed.

The sense of relief almost overwhelmed him.

He exhaled slowly before turning back to Parnell. His hands clenched into fists, and it took all of his willpower not to lunge. He'd never before experienced the urge to do serious bodily harm, but the fear in Nikki's eyes released in him a primitive urge to wrap his hands around the kid's throat and slowly choke the life out of him.

Unfortunately, giving in to the urge could have disastrous consequences if Parnell decided to actually use that gun in his hand.

"Whatever this is about," he said, attempting to sound reasonable, "it has nothing to do with Nikki."

Parnell rubbed his jaw. "I'm not entirely convinced of that fact."

"This is between you and me. Let her go."

Parnell tilted his head, as if considering for a moment. Then he shook his head. "I don't think so."

"Why not?"

"Because she's obviously important to you, or you wouldn't have broken land-speed records to get here."

"I'm only interested in making sure nobody gets hurt," Colin said.

"You were married to her once."

"A long time ago," he said.

"You were with her in Pennsylvania."

Colin didn't know how Parnell could know that, but he didn't dare deny it. He shrugged, deliberately nonchalant. "I was lonely. She was available."

He couldn't look at Nikki. He didn't want to see how she might react to his callous dismissal of everything they'd shared over the past few weeks. He could only hope that he'd get a chance to explain, and that she would understand.

"She really doesn't mean anything to you?"

Colin shrugged again, hoping against hope that his cavalier attitude would succeed in getting Parnell to let Nikki go. He didn't care if she didn't let him explain, if she hated him forever, as long as she was alive to do so. "We had some good times."

Parnell considered for a moment. "That's a good story," he said at last. "Except for one thing."

The faint stirring of hope faded. "What's that?"

"She came all the way to Texas to see you."

"I didn't ask her to come," Colin said quickly. "I didn't even know she was here until you called."

Parnell pointed the gun at him. "Don't lie to me."

"He didn't know I was coming."

Nikki's blurted admission succeeded in drawing Parnell's attention away from Colin and back to her, which was exactly what Colin had been trying to avoid.

"Then why are you here?" Parnell demanded.

"Colin left Pennsylvania rather abruptly," she said. "I wanted to see him again...to clear up a possible misunderstanding."

"What kind of misunderstanding?"

She finally turned and met his gaze. He didn't have any trouble reading the emotions in her eyes this time: regret, fear, love.

"There was something I forgot to tell you before you left," she said softly.

He knew what she was going to say, and at any other time he would have been overjoyed to hear the words. But now, an admission of her feelings could get her killed.

"There's nothing left to say," he interrupted harshly, silently begging her to back off.

But her gaze never flickered. "I came to Texas for a reason," she told him. "This may be my last chance, so I'm going to say it. I love you, Colin."

The joy at hearing her finally speak those words filled his heart, as did the terror of what Parnell would do with this information.

"Ahh," Parnell mocked. "Isn't that sweet?"

He turned to Colin, a triumphant gleam in his eye. "Now I want to hear you say it, Coach. I want to know how you really feel about this woman."

It was an effort to tear his eyes away from Nikki, but he forced himself to do so. If Parnell had even a hint of his true feelings for Nikki, it would all be over.

"I feel sorry for her," Colin said. "She obviously can't let go of the past. She can't accept that whatever feelings I had for her died a long time ago."

Parnell's eyes narrowed dangerously. "Wrong answer."

Then he pulled the trigger.

Chapter 18

"That was to get your attention. To let you know that I'm not afraid to use this gun."

Parnell was pleased that his voice was calm, despite the fact that the recoil from the shot had startled him. He looked from the hole in the wall to McIver to the woman and back again. McIver's face had gone positively ashen and the woman's eyes were filled with tears.

He smiled. "Now tell the truth, Coach, or the next bullet may be fatal."

McIver swallowed, glanced helplessly at the woman.

Before he could speak, the phone on the desk began to shrill.

Parnell jolted at the sound.

It rang again. Dammit, how was he supposed to think with this kind of interruption? He snatched up the receiver with his free hand.

"What?"

"Duncan Parnell?" a cool voice asked.

He muttered a curse, wondering how anyone could have tracked him down here. "Who's asking?"

"It's Detective Brock with the Austin P.D.," the caller informed him. "We heard a shot fired inside and wanted to make sure everyone was okay in there."

Sweat beaded on his upper lip as the implications of the cop's words sank in. He stretched the phone cord over to the window. Looking through the slats of the blinds, he saw at least a dozen police cars parked outside the building. Dammit, this was *not* part of his plan.

"Is everyone okay?" Brock asked again.

"What the hell business is it of yours?"

"I want to negotiate with you for the release of the hostages," the cop said patiently. "But first I need to know that they're unharmed."

Sweat trickled into his eyes, stinging them. He blinked fiercely, as his mind grasped for a way to salvage the situation.

"We have the building surrounded," Brock warned him. "There are snipers on the roof across the street."

He was bluffing. Even if there were snipers, Parnell was confident they wouldn't be able to target him through the blinds. From outside, they'd only be able to see shadows. They wouldn't risk shooting McIver or the woman by mistake.

"The only way for you to get out of there alive is to release the hostages and surrender."

Parnell shook his head. No way in hell was he going to surrender. This was *his* show and he'd be damned before he'd let anyone take him off center stage.

"They're not hostages," he told the cop. "They're victims. And the only thing left to negotiate is which one will die first."

He slammed down the phone.

* * *

Colin flinched, his last hope that he and Nikki would get out of there alive decimated by Parnell's words.

"You must have thought you were pretty clever," Parnell snarled at him. "Bringing the cops in."

"I was trying to help you."

Parnell's laugh was derisive. "Like you were helping when you benched me?"

"Even Gil saw that you were too messed up to be playing."

Parnell faltered for just a second. "Gil?"

"He's the one who told me about the pills."

"Bullshit. Gil wouldn't betray me. It was Jonesy—Jonesy figured he could have my slot if you pulled me from the line-up."

"It was Gil," Colin said again. "And he told me because he was worried about you."

"You're lying," Parnell said again, sounding just a little desperate now. "It was Jonesy. You and Jonesy ruined my career. Now it's time for payback."

He leveled the gun at Colin.

"Think about this, Parnell," Colin was openly pleading now. "You won't get out of here alive if you start shooting."

"I only need one shot," Parnell said, and he turned the gun toward Nikki. "For her."

Please, God, no.

Colin had never been a particularly religious man, but he was praying fervently now.

"It will be even better than killing you," Parnell told him. "Because you'll suffer more watching the life bleed out of the woman you love than you would by dying."

He was going to pull the trigger.

Looking into his cold dark eyes, Nikki didn't doubt it

for a second. Duncan Parnell was going to pull the trigger
again, and this time she was going to die.

Fear paralyzed her for half a second, until she remembered why she'd come to Texas today. She wasn't going
to give up.

She needed that determination now more than ever.
She refused to let Duncan Parnell destroy their hopes for
a future together or make their little girl an orphan. She
wasn't going to let him win.

She bent her knees and braced her bound feet against
the desk.

He leveled the gun at her, his finger nestled against
the trigger.

Nikki took one last breath and pushed against the desk.

Colin launched himself toward Parnell.

The echo of the second shot had barely sounded before
the window shattered in an explosion of glass. Colin fell
backward with Parnell and was pinned momentarily by
the kid's weight.

He struggled to his feet, frantic to get to Nikki. He'd
heard the shot, watched in horror as her chair flipped
over. She'd obviously been hit, but where and how badly
he didn't know.

He didn't spare a glance for Parnell's prone form or
the two crimson stains that bloomed on the front of his
shirt, then slowly bled together. The only thing that mattered was Nikki.

"Nic?" He ran his hands over her, frantically searching for any sign of injury, any hint of blood.

Her eyelids flickered, opened.

"My head hurts," she murmured.

His relief was so overwhelming he almost laughed.
"You must have hit it on the filing cabinet."

He glanced at the metal cabinet, now dented where the
chair had slammed into it as it tipped over. His blood

froze as he saw another, smaller indentation only a few inches above.

He tore his gaze from the bullet hole. He wouldn't even consider how differently this situation might have ended. Instead, he framed Nikki's face in his trembling hands and silently thanked God for answering his prayers.

"Colin?" Nikki said hesitantly. "Are you okay?"

He managed a smile. "Yeah."

There was so much more he wanted to say, so much he needed to tell her, but suddenly the room was swarming with police and crime-scene technicians and medical personnel and he and Nikki were separated to be interviewed about what had happened.

When Nikki found Colin again, he was standing beside one of the police cruisers, shaking hands with a man she'd earlier learned was Detective Brock. He spotted her in the same instant, and they met in the middle of the parking lot.

"About the things I said in there," Colin began, nodding toward his office.

"I know you didn't mean them," she said.

"What about the things *you* said in there?"

She smiled. "I meant every word."

Then she raised herself onto her toes and touched her mouth to his.

Nikki might have initiated the kiss, but Colin took control of it almost immediately. His lips crushed down on hers, hot and hungry, blazingly possessive. She felt the earth spin in dizzying circles as she clung to him, kissing him back with a passion that matched his own.

Slowly the edge of desperation subsided. The bruising pressure of his mouth eased, the arm banded tightly around her loosened. But still he kissed her. Softly, sweetly, lovingly.

Nikki sighed contentedly. "I do love you—"

"Colin. Finally."

He cursed under his breath at being interrupted, then again when he looked up and saw the source. "My agent," he explained to Nikki, turning away from her with obvious reluctance.

"I've been all over this place looking for you," Ian said.

"And as usual," Colin told him, "your timing sucks."

Nikki stepped back, out of the warmth of his embrace, to give them some measure of privacy.

"You won't think so when I tell you what I've got." Ian grinned, waving a sheaf of papers in front of him.

"How did you even know I was here?"

"The hostage thing was on the news," his agent said.

Colin shook his head. "You know what happened in there, and still you tracked me down to talk about a damn contract?"

Ian huffed indignantly. "Will you at least look at it before you reject it?"

"No." He shook his head again. "I'm not going to sign."

Nikki could no longer pretend she wasn't listening. She couldn't let him make what would obviously be a huge mistake. "What do you mean—you're not going to sign?"

He turned to her. "I thought you'd be on my side here."

"How could you ever think I'd want you to give up something that means so much to you?"

"You and Carly mean a whole lot more," he told her. "I want us to be together, to be a real family."

It was what she'd wanted to hear for so long, but she still couldn't let him make this kind of sacrifice. "We can do that in Texas."

"You would move here?"

"I'd go to the ends of the earth to be with you," she said. "All that matters is that we're together."

"Do you really mean that?"

"With all my heart."

Colin pulled her back into his arms and planted a firm kiss on her lips.

Beside him, Ian exhaled an audible sigh of relief. "Does that mean you'll finally sign?"

He drew back from Nikki, grinning. "No."

"But—"

Colin was quick to cut off his agent's protest. "No," he said again.

"You're making a huge mistake," Ian grumbled.

"It's my mistake to make."

"You won't ever see another offer like this again."

"I don't care." He smiled at Nikki, making her believe that he really meant it.

Muttering under his breath, Ian unzipped his briefcase and shoved the papers Colin had rejected inside.

"Let me know when you have something from Channel 12," he said.

His agent shot him a narrow-eyed look before he withdrew a legal-size envelope from his case and passed it to Colin.

Nikki watched the exchange with apparent bafflement.

"What are you doing?" she finally ventured to ask.

"Just trust me on this." He opened the envelope and withdrew what was obviously a contract of some kind. He scanned the contents only briefly before nodding his approval.

"Give me a pen."

Ian did as he was instructed, shaking his head the whole while.

Colin signed all three copies of the contract, then handed the package back to his agent.

She waited until his agent had moved away, still muttering under his breath, before she asked, "Are you going to tell me what that was about?"

He grinned. "As of now, I am Fairweather Cable's newest sports commentator."

Her jaw fell open. "You gave up coaching for a desk job?"

"It's not a desk job," he chided. "It's television."

"But…why?"

"Because even if you and Carly were here, I'd be on the road with the team so much that we'd hardly ever see each other. And because I don't ever want to spend a single minute more than I have to with you out of my sight again."

"But…" She wanted to run after his departing agent, to tear up the contracts Colin had signed, because despite the conviction in his words and the sincerity of his tone, she was so afraid he'd someday regret what he'd just done. "But you love coaching."

"It's not what I want," he told her. "Not anymore."

"You better be very sure of this, Colin. I don't ever want you to regret—"

He touched a finger to her lips. "The only thing I've ever regretted is the time we were apart.

"I love you, Nicole, more than I ever thought it was possible to love someone. And I want to be with you forever."

His unwavering certainty stilled the questions in her heart.

"I love Carly, too," he said. "And I want to spend time with her. I want to watch out for her and watch her grow.

"I want us to have other children together. I want to see the changes your body goes through during pregnancy. I want to hold your hand during labor, and watch you nurse our baby. I want to be there when he or she cuts a first tooth, takes a first step, speaks a first word.

"But most of all, I just want to share my life with you. I want to go to sleep beside you every night and wake up beside you every morning. If you'll give me another chance, I'll spend every day of the rest of my life showing you how much I love you."

It was the longest speech she'd ever heard him make, and Nikki wasn't prepared for the wealth of emotion that swept over her. This was so much more than she'd ever expected. More than she'd ever dared hope for. Everything she'd ever dreamed of.

Then, just when she thought he couldn't surprise her any more, he dropped down to one knee on the hard asphalt, in the middle of the now near-empty parking lot.

"Will you marry me, Nicole?"

She wasn't sure she could answer, wasn't sure she could even breathe. She swallowed. "You didn't say anything about diapers."

"Diapers?" Colin frowned.

She nodded. "If we have any more children, you'll have to agree to take your turn changing diapers."

Some of the tension seemed to ease from his body. "I promise to take my turn changing diapers."

Nikki took a deep breath and prepared to leap. "Then I'll marry you."

Colin whooped with joy and scooped her into his arms. He swung her around, and laughter bubbled up inside of her, spilled over. Just like the love that was overflowing in her heart.

He set her back on her feet but kept one arm around her as he fished the ring out of his pocket with the other hand.

"You must have been pretty sure I'd say yes."

He grinned. "The only thing I was sure of was that I wasn't going to stop asking until you did."

Nikki chuckled softly and held out her hand to him. Her fingers weren't quite steady, but neither, she noticed, were his. He paused with the circle of gold and diamonds at her fingertip.

"Be very sure of this," he said, turning her words back on her. "This time I won't settle for any less than forever."

She helped him push the ring onto her finger. "This time, neither will I."

*   *   *   *   *

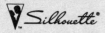

INTIMATE MOMENTS™

**Coming in April 2004
from**

MELISSA JAMES

Dangerous Illusion
(Silhouette Intimate Moments #1288)

Secret agent Brendan McCall is assigned his most difficult mission: he must find and protect a woman who may or may not be the runaway wife of a dangerous international villain—and the woman he once loved and lost. Brendan can save Beth Silver's life...but will he succeed at winning her heart?

*Available April 2004
at your favorite
retail outlet.*

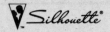

eHARLEQUIN.com

Looking for today's most popular
books at great prices?
At www.eHarlequin.com, we offer:

- An **extensive selection** of romance
  books by top authors!

- **New** releases, Themed Collections
  and hard-to-find **backlist.**

- A sneak peek at Upcoming books.

- Enticing book **excerpts** and **back
  cover copy!**

- Read recommendations from other
  readers (and post your own)!

- Find out what everybody's reading
  in **Bestsellers.**

- **Save BIG** with everyday discounts
  and exclusive online offers!

- Easy, convenient **24-hour shopping.**

- Our **Romance Legend** will help select
  reading that's *exactly* right for you!

**Your purchases are 100%
guaranteed—so shop online
at www.eHarlequin.com today!**

If you enjoyed what you just read,
then we've got an offer you can't resist!

Take 2 bestselling
love stories FREE!
Plus get a FREE surprise gift!